Runaway Wallflower

RUNAWAY WALLFLOWER

Bianca Blythe

Contents

Chapter One

H is men were not going to like this.

Rupert strode over the deck of *The Sapphire Princess*, clutching the letter Arthur Carmichael had given him.

"Listen!" Rupert's voice boomed over the crashing of azure waves against the hull. "I have an announcement."

"Aye, Cap'n."

Some pirates clambered down the rigging, and others stepped over the rope strewn deck to reach him. Gold gleamed from some of their fingers. Their last haul had been bloody magnificent.

"Reckon 'e's found us another ship to attack." Fergus brushed his fingers through his red beard, the length wilder and more unrestrained than anything the Royal Navy would allow. "Practice your figures, men. We'll be counting jewels soon."

The other pirates cheered at the sailor's musings, and their eyes sparkled as their lips spread into toothy grins. They rubbed their hands and even ceased their incessant tobacco chewing.

"What be it, Cap'n? Spanish? Portuguese?" Fergus asked. "Don't suppose it's...French?"

"Nah." A pirate shook his head, and his gold earrings shimmered in the sunlight. "Can't be that. We've chased them all away!"

Laughter rumbled and drowned the thunder of waves and wind.

"We are going to England," Rupert announced.

"You be asking us to attack our home country?" One pirate hollered, and his bottom lip managed to drop to a level it didn't even reach when gobbling meat pie. "His Majesty's own territories?"

The other pirates quieted, and the waves seemed to once again roar. Salty spray toppled onto the deck, as if Neptune himself were contemplating sinking *The Sapphire Princess* at the sound of such heresy.

"Ain't all of our country." Fergus glared at the patriotic pirate. "Some of us be hating that land. Stealing good Cornish stock."

A few others murmured. Fergus wasn't the only man to have been impressed into the Royal Navy.

Fergus placed a roughened hand over his chest. "Don't ye worry, Cap'n. I'll be helping you attack England. Jes you see. Reckon the pistols work the same on the English as they do on those frogs."

"While I appreciate your loyalty, that won't be necessary," Rupert said. "I have something else in mind. We will no longer attack anybody."

"Never?" Confusion riddled the faces of his men. "But how will we survive? We gotta eat, Cap'n."

"We will become tradesmen. Merchants."

The men frowned. Some tilted their heads, as if a new

angle for their ears might change the words ushered from Rupert's lips.

"We will become..." Rupert sighed, and even his chest tightened at the words he would need to say next. "Decent people."

Horror scudded over his crew's faces.

"My word." Fergus strode toward him. "Perhaps 'e's 'ad too much sun. Bound to 'appen 'ere in the West Indies. Jes never thought it would 'appen to the Cap'n. Now bless your 'eart, Cap'n. You sure you don't wanna lie down?"

"I do not take orders from the weather," Rupert growled. "If any one of you desire to remain pirates, I will understand. I'm certain when we stop in Port Royale that you'll find another captain to work for given all of your impeccable qualifications for causing havoc on the oceans."

"Ain't nobody that ain't affeared of *The Sapphire Princess*. 'Specially you, Cap'n Brown Beard," Fergus said, and the rest of his crew shouted assent. "Yer the scariest captain of them all."

Pride swept through Rupert, but he limited himself to a solemn nod. "You shouldn't call me that anymore. I doubt other tradesmen will desire to part with their goods to a man with that appellation."

"But what shall we call you?"

He hesitated. There was his birth name of course, but he hadn't gone completely mad, despite what the others might think of him. He sighed. "You may call me, Captain Rosse."

He thrummed his hand through his beard. It had taken years for him to grow it to its current bushy and intimidating length. "I'll be shaving this anyway. You'll all need to get cleaned up too."

"I suppose I'm jes a regular sailor now," Fergus lamented. "Ah, it's an end of an era."

Rupert glanced again at the sophisticated script that formed the letter's signature. "It's the beginning of a better one. Men, set the sails for Brighton!"

Chapter Two

Brighton
  July 1817

Louisa's mother may have suggested they visit the English Channel, but Louisa was certain her mother had not intended her to venture *into* it.

At least, not without a sturdy horse to haul her bathing machine into a sufficiently deep portion of the water, and certainly not without two trained guides to thrust her from the machine. Sisters of dukes were not supposed to be visible to the telescope-wielding gentlemen who strolled the shore for glimpses of young ladies in flannel bathing costumes.

She would forego any chaperone, even the imposing four-legged variety.

Raindrops continued to topple downward, and pebbles glistened on the shore, abetted by the constant drizzle. Gray waves lapped against the shore and mirrored the gray sky. It might be afternoon, but the sun seemed to have vanished long ago. She'd spent her whole season looking forward to when she'd next be by the ocean, but British weather hadn't failed to accompany her. *Still.* The familiar scent of the sea was unmistakable, and her lips ascended upward.

Chalky cliffs adorned with sheep curved around the town, and ships squatted on the horizon. The town lacked a proper harbor, though that did not dissuade ships from anchoring. Loutish sailors sat in cutters and sloshed their oars through the foamy waves in rhythm.

Beside her, chaises and barouches rumbled past ivory townhouses so new the salt spray scarcely sullied their elegant exteriors, and tourists thronged below the domes of the Marine Palace. They fixed their gazes on the structure, as if hopeful the regent would declare a passion for rainy weather and abandon his sumptuous sanctuary to join them outside.

"You shouldn't be doing this, miss." Raindrops dappled Becky's cap, the coarse cotton and single lace ribbon an ineffectual barrier against the drizzle. "And you mustn't forget that your mother desires to speak with you."

Louisa swallowed the self-reproach that surged through her. "I must. It's my last chance."

Their feet crunched over the shingle screen that protected Brighton's shore, and Louisa refrained from informing Becky that she had another errand after this.

"Be careful," Becky said.

"I'm simply going swimming," Louisa said, though they both knew nothing about her activity could be characterized as normal.

The wind swept against Louisa with more than its customary vigor, and seaweed lay scattered over the ocean, creating a soggy border that only a few valiant seagulls ventured to dip into.

And me.

On another day the thought might make her smile, but today she only clutched her diving helmet more tightly.

This is the last time.

She placed her diving helmet over her head and fastened it to the collar that accompanied it. She'd designed the helmet herself, selecting the copper material that would withstand water.

She handed the long leather hoses attached to the helmet to her maid. One hose supplied air to the back of the helmet, and used air exited from a similar pipe in the front.

Becky's expression did not echo the joy that cascaded through Louisa. "You resemble some sort of soldier, miss. You're fortunate somebody hasn't shot you."

"I would never permit that to happen," Louisa said, though the words came out muffled. The waves rippled temptingly before her, and the salty scent filled her nostrils.

She inhaled and stepped into the gray waves. She strove to memorize the sound of her feet crunching against pebbles and the crisp temperature that energized her body. Murky shadows of jellyfish flitted about, content to indulge in the water constantly, and not spurred by a pressing inclination to escape their relatives.

She strode deeper into the ocean, her strides made more inelegant than normal by her heavy bathing costume. The water rippled into tempting billows, but she raised her head to the horizon.

Steel clouds rolled over the sky, their speed unhampered by the weight of their yet unreleased ammunition. Below them the dark outlines of ships heading to larger ports flitted through the billowing waves, the crests larger and more turbulent than that expected for a seaside town at the height of summer.

Raindrops fell with greater speed, and few bathers ventured into the water. Only a smattering of defiant tourists, perhaps determined to attain all of Brighton's offerings after their likely uncomfortable coach ride through the copiously clay laden lanes of the Weald, hovered beside their bathing machines.

Some sailors rowed passengers to the large ships anchored outside the city. Brighton might not have a proper harbor, but it was still a town of ever-growing importance. Most were likely headed to the ship bound for Dieppe, but Louisa allowed her gaze to rest on a larger ship. *The Sapphire Princess.*

Nothing about the schooner indicated it was bound for the West Indies, but Louisa still inhaled, as if she might smell the scent of pineapples and tropical flowers.

She flickered her eyelids down, and her mind envisioned turquoise water and cerulean skies. Warm, salty waves might crest about her, and she almost felt the flutter of palm trees and glimpsed their unchanging, consistent colors and their wide leaves that feathered delicate shadows over the sand.

Were the fish in the Caribbean truly as different as everyone said? Were they simply more colorful versions of the trout and haddock with which she was familiar? Or did they possess structural variations unique to those islands? And if that was the case, as she suspected, how could that happen?

Some Renaissance scientists had interested themselves in such matters, but the information was outdated. Louisa desired data, and her diving helmet would make the gathering of such information verge on the effortless.

Tomorrow Mr. Thornton, a man who met all the requirements of athleticism demanded for a diver coupled with scholarly ability, would change the ichthyological field, and she would be able to say she performed a small function in aiding him. She couldn't wait to meet him.

Louisa sank into the frigid water before any of the other bathers might exclaim at the oddity of her contraption. She welcomed her descent, shivering only slightly, intent on enjoying her last minutes with the diving helmet. Water remained her preferred place to be, but ever since her mother had read a certain unflattering article, it was the only place of any tolerance.

Especially now.

Her eyes no longer hurt when she peered under the surface, her chest no longer ached as it fought for air despite her desire to prolong her time underwater, and her hair no longer obscured her view when she swam: her diving helmet rendered such problems obsolete.

Some fish stilled, as if sensing her presence, but she wasn't going to harm them.

This was Louisa's world, one where no one chided her for being too shy or awkward.

She swam through seaweed, and brown shrimp skirted away from her. Mussels, clams, and cockles dotted the ocean floor, their pearly shells gleaming from the dark sand. Large yellow starfish gripped hold of rocks, as if conscious of the comfort of their position and to hinder a frightful fate of being swept up to the surface. Crabs stepped daintily over the mussels, undeterred by their high leg count, and Louisa smiled.

If only this were not the last time.

She'd spent so long fabricating her diving helmet, and it would take her months to reconstruct it. The copper exterior, inspired from those worn by men fighting fires, had needed to be commissioned especially. She'd found men suspicious of doing business with women, and she would need to wait for one of her brothers to return for her request to be given sufficient respect. Even a small flaw in the diving helmet could be perilous.

Percival was in Sussex with his new bride and baby, and Arthur was in Jamaica again on some undisclosed business.

She sighed. At least Mr. Thornton would be able to make good use of the helmet in the Caribbean. There were likely all sorts of fish to document there. Tonight she would meet him, and all her hopes for her research would come true.

"Miss Carmichael! Miss Carmichael!" A high-pitched voice interrupted her contemplation.

Louisa's stomach tumbled inelegantly, and she lifted her head over the surface of the water.

"Miss Carmichael!" Her maid's voice bellowed through the air, the strength uncommon in women of her profession, though one which Louisa's mother announced as foremost in a quality to make her a good hire.

Becky hurried toward her, dragging her hem through the ocean as her brown curls tumbled from her white cap. A group of infirm patients who were being urged by their caretakers toward the sea, likely driven by various doctors' assurances that the sensation of icy waves would snap them into sanity, stared at them.

"You've been in the water for thirty minutes, miss," Becky announced. "And your mother—"

Louisa swallowed back a sigh and forced herself to smile. "Thank you for informing me."

She strode toward Becky, even though the waves still pushed against her, urging her to fling herself back into the sea.

A few caretakers glanced in her direction, as if to assess whether she might become their next charge, before continuing to berate their patients' reluctance to enter the frigid waters. They remained resolved to be seen as attempting to cure their charges' ailments, likely lest their patients' wealthy relatives cease their substantial payments.

Louisa marched past them, striving to ignore the sharp chilliness that pervaded her and intensified as her wet attire rubbed against her skin. She handed the diving helmet into Becky's hands. "Take extreme care."

"I wish I hadn't had to hurry you, miss. But your mother did request your presence."

Becky accompanied her to one of the tiny buildings on the shore relegated to changing, and Louisa darted inside to slip on a dress. At least her hair remained dry, and she hurried toward Becky. "We need to board a ship. I'm delivering the diving helmet to the scientist who will conduct his research with it."

Becky was too well-trained to remind Louisa that her mother would disapprove, but her eyes *did* widen, and her eyebrows *did* clamber up her freckled face.

"It's important," Louisa said.

She wrapped her arms around her waist and pressed her hands against the tangerine-colored fabric her mother had chosen for her afternoon dress. Louisa was still damp from her swim, and the brisk wind chilled her further.

They headed toward the boats that departed between

Ship Street and Middle Street, and Louisa ignored the questioning gazes of the fishermen. They grasped hold of their fishing nets and poles, signifiers that they'd marked their territory, and she absolutely did not belong here.

Finally they reached Ship Street. She addressed one man in a shore boat who seemed to be taking people across and paid the fare.

"Come, Becky," Louisa said.

Her maid shifted her legs and tightened her hold on a wooden pole despite the unappealing shades of green that crept over it.

"This won't take long," Louisa said. "But I could go alone—"

Becky's skin seemed to leap several degrees in paleness, and she scrambled into the boat. "I—I couldn't let you do that, miss. I wouldn't be doing my duty."

Her voice reached such a mournful note that worry swept through Louisa. "Are you ill? Is it the boat? Not everyone likes the water—"

"It's not that, miss." Becky bit her lip, and she clutched her fingers together. "*I'm* well. I promise."

"Then I be off now," the rower said. He clonked his oars into the water and pushed off. "This is what 'appens with women going on ships alone. Jes ain't right. Not what the good Lord intended, that's for sure." He frowned at them. "Can you point out in the Bible where women got into ships by themselves?"

"Given that the greater portion of the Bible is set in the desert, ships would seem to be rather superfluous," Louisa replied.

The question seemed to belong to the rhetorical variety, for the man simply laughed and concentrated on rowing them across to where the ship was anchored.

Becky scooted closer to Louisa, and when she spoke, her voice was low. "Nobody has any business being on *The Sapphire Princess*. Least of all a woman like yourself. You're lucky if they don't kidnap you and hold you for ransom." Becky's voice took on an awestruck quality, as if already rehearsing telling people of that occurrence.

It was almost enough to make Louisa smile.

Almost.

She frowned. "It's just a ship, Becky. We'll be on one later when we return to America."

"That ain't no ship," Becky said. Her cheeks flushed. "Isn't. Pardon, miss."

"What do you mean?" Louisa's voice wobbled, and she glanced again in the direction of the imposing hull, adorned with three majestic masts.

"Don't you know how the captain got hold of it?"

"No." Louisa's stomach tightened uncomfortably.

"He won it," Becky said, and her voice now definitely emanated awe. "In a *pirate* raid."

"That's nonsense," Louisa said.

"Is it?"

"It's just sitting in the bay. You would think somebody would arrest him, if—"

"You think the regent don't fancy fine goods? Pineapples and rum? Sugar and coffee? Reckon if 'e's a pirate, he wouldn't be needing to force the regent to pay the outrageous tariffs everyone complains about. Besides..." Becky tossed her head, "...there's a reason why he's docked in Brighton."

"Oh?" Louisa may have had an alto voice, but it was decidedly approaching soprano territory.

"Reckon the captain likes that he can make a quick getaway."

"Nonsense. Everyone knows the Thames is ridiculously crowded. I'm sure he's really being quite sensible staying here." Louisa gave her most adamant nod, even as her voice faltered.

"Perhaps," Becky said, but her tone indicated a belief that she assigned only the slimmest likelihood that Louisa might be correct.

Louisa's stomach toppled downward, and she needed to remind herself that the waves were wobbling the boat, and the world was not truly quivering about her.

Her plan remained. She would give the diving helmet to Mr. Thornton and then she would be off. Later she might discuss the matter more with him at the ball.

She clutched her diving helmet closer to her. Some days the ocean sparkled. Other days the foam crests of the waves dazzled under the force of the sun.

Today was not one of those days.

Chapter Three

Rupert did not habitually sprawl over the ship's surface, but *The Sapphire Princess* remained mostly empty. The cargo and provisions were loaded, and the men were exploring Brighton, even if the town didn't promise to satisfy the sailors' Dionysian instincts, indulged and strengthened by their frequent stops in the West Indies.

Rupert missed the customary dip and swerve of the ship. Life seemed less enthralling when the ship was still. Mr. Thornton, a scientist who would be sailing with them to the West Indies, was late.

His lips twitched. He'd never had to worry about late passengers when he was a pirate. Any passengers had embarked on *The Sapphire Princess* against their will, and they'd quickly pledged to join his crew under the gleeful pressure of Fergus and his own more somber and intimidating duress. Clearly respectability involved greater challenges.

Fergus frowned. "It ain't right that we're 'ere now. 'Tis no country for good folks."

"It is our own country," Rupert reminded Fergus, but he shook his head.

"No, it ain't and you know it. 'Tis no proper country that forced us into the navy at a young age."

Rupert's smile wobbled as Fergus reminded him of the once-told lie. Perhaps the British ships had shown up at Fergus's secluded hamlet in Cornwall, but that was not how Rupert joined.

No matter.

Fergus didn't need to know how Rupert came to be working beside him.

Rupert rose. "I'm going to work in my quarters."

Fergus nodded solemnly. "Aye, it's raining. Never should have come 'ere. We don't 'ave to deliver fine furniture from England when we could 'ave been delivering perfectly respectable timber and dried cod from Massachusetts and Rhode Island. Not quite as exciting as being a pirate, but I suppose it's nice not to worry each day is our last."

"Next journey, Fergus." Rupert smiled. "It was either here or Scotland, and I doubt you would have appreciated that land's even lower temperature.

"Scotland!" Fergus scrunched his forehead. "I don't mean no disrespect, but I'm sure you've gone mad!"

"Not that, Fergus. Do not fear." Rupert rose and glanced at the expensive townhomes that made up Brighton's skyline along with the peregrine domes of the Marine Pavilion. Elegantly attired people paced the parade, their footsteps brisker than Rupert suspected the occasion demanded. Everything seemed overly pompous in this town.

Or rather...almost everything.

A tall, slender woman in an orange dress marched on

the parade. Thick auburn locks cascaded unbecomingly over her back, as if she'd crushed them underneath a hat.

Not that she was wearing a hat.

He sighed. Her hair was not the important part. Rupert didn't make a habit of pondering women's hairstyles, even if this one seemed remarkably poorly conceived.

He noticed her because she was hauling a huge, awkward package and a maid, evidenced by the stark black dress and white apron, scurried after her.

It may have been a while since Rupert had visited England, if not quite as long as he'd told Fergus, but he doubted women had taken to carry things rather than their servants.

He frowned and descended the steep steps that led beneath the deck. No need to ponder the idiosyncrasies of women.

He strode through the corridor and entered his quarters. Various luxuries glinted from the walls. Polished silver gleamed from the mahogany cabinet bolted to the wall for dinners with important passengers the ship never carried. Pastel paintings of the French countryside, a nod to the ship's last captain, hung on the walls, and carved furniture dotted the room.

Rupert grinned. Perhaps if the past captain had interested himself less in art and more in studying defense tactics, he would not have succumbed so quickly to Rupert's crew.

Rupert wasn't unaccustomed to finery, but this room surpassed his previous sumptuous surroundings and served as a paragon of what he'd achieved: himself, and not some accident of birth. Unlike the army, where wealthy parents were prone to purchase their sons commissions in safe regiments, the navy remained a meritocracy. Sailing a ship required intricate knowledge, and the Royal Navy, the very best navy in the world, was not going to allow anyone to have charge of a ship without respecting the person's talents.

No matter how extreme the circumstances of the person's birth.

His lips twitched, and he sat at his desk and removed his ledger. He might no longer be a member of the Royal Navy, but he still respected the skills it had taught him. He added new details from the sojourn in Brighton, and his shoulders relaxed as he inspected the carefully inscribed black numbers.

A knock sounded on the door, and he set aside his quill. "Enter."

The door swung open, and Fergus trudged in. "There be someone to see you, Cap'n."

Probably a merchant. Rupert straightened his jacket. This could be good. Very good. "Show him in."

"It's a—woman, actually."

"A *woman?*"

Fergus gave a forlorn look.

"You shouldn't bother me with this," Rupert grumbled. "You know we don't allow women on board."

"She was—er—rather insistent. You know 'ow they get." Fergus frowned, and Rupert removed his gaze from the sailor's face. It wouldn't do for Fergus to see him smile.

Fergus wasn't the only sailor to find women intimidating.

"She's on the deck, Cap'n."

"Hmph." At least Fergus hadn't brought her to his quarters, lest she start undressing for him.

He'd experienced that before. And though he wasn't immune to the charms of women, he wanted to preserve a sense of order on the ship. If word reached his sailors that he'd entertained a woman of the night, while forbidding them the same, he'd risk losing some of that crucial respect.

"We're not that kind of ship." Rupert stood and exited his quarters, pondering what kind of harlot would be waiting for him. He set his mouth into a grim line and marched through the narrow corridors. He didn't have time for this. He climbed the steep staircase to the deck, pounding his feet against the wooden steps.

He was accustomed to them at other ports. Some thought meeting the sailors on their boats would be easy money. And in truth, they were probably correct—in most cases.

But Rupert's aspirations wouldn't be fulfilled if he was given the reputation for indecency. His pirate days were in the past, and the companies he wanted to work for prided themselves on respectability. This was his first journey shipping British goods to Barbados and Jamaica. Rupert had no urge to captain one of the slave-hauling ships, and he didn't desire his men to find themselves working on one either.

He fixed his face into a scowl and marched over the deck.

Two women stood before him, though neither possessed the garish flourish he'd expected.

He recognized them at once.

The woman in the tangerine dress stood before him, clutching a bulky packet that extended from her arms to her face. At least her maid had the decency to look abashed.

"I'm afraid we do not allow women on this ship," he said.

"So we were informed." The woman in orange darted an unpleased look in the direction of Fergus.

"Yet here you are."

"I'm delivering a package." A faint American accent flitted through her voice.

He gave her a hard stare, but her cheeks did not pinken, and she did not swing her gaze away from him.

She was the strangest messenger he'd ever seen, but he wouldn't give her the satisfaction of informing her. The woman might find his mention of her uniqueness flattering.

He nodded at the awkward package she was clutching. "I take it that's for me."

"For your passenger," she said. "Mr. Sebastian Thornton, the esteemed scientist. Where is he? I demand to speak to him."

He frowned. "And what is your name?"

The woman in the orange dress hesitated.

"My name is irrelevant," she said finally.

"This is my ship, and I'll decide what's relevant." Rupert narrowed the distance between them. More than one person had told him the sound of his boots striking the wooden deck resembled gunfire, and he resisted the urge to smile at the maid's predictable paling. He might no longer wear a bushy beard and earrings, but he hadn't forgotten how to intimidate.

He cast a smug look in the direction of the orange-clad woman, eager to witness her capitulation, but she only cast a stony look toward him.

He frowned, and the maid's eyes widened further. "She's—she's 'is sister!"

The orange-clad woman frowned, but his lips moved into a smile. This was how things should be.

"Very well, Miss Thornton."

"I demand to speak with him," she said.

He frowned. People were not supposed to make demands of him, especially when standing upon his ship. "He's not here."

The woman blinked, and her expression appeared rather less defiant. "But you are bound for the West Indies."

He nodded.

"And this is *The Sapphire Princess?*" She cast a look in the direction of the rower, as if he might have brought her to the wrong ship.

"It is indeed."

"Oh." Worry flitted over her face, but she soon composed herself. "Well then, he is bound to arrive soon."

"Perhaps he decided to wait to board the ship until tomorrow," Rupert said. "Since that is of course when the ship actually departs."

"He said he would be here."

"Then he is tardy." He must not have managed to conjure up requisite enthusiasm for this man, for the woman frowned.

"You are very lucky to have him. His research will be most groundbreaking. Everyone will know the name of the ship."

"I'm not seeking fame."

In fact, he was avoiding it.

"Every scientist will know, I mean." This time the woman's face did flush, but she sterned her expression before he could decide whether her pinkening cheeks were an improvement.

"When every scientist takes to importing cargo to the West Indies," Rupert said, "I will be most grateful."

The woman gave him a tight smile. The woman's avid laudations of her brother did not dissuade him from his distaste of overly educated toffs. This man was not even on time. Sailors were much more reasonable.

"Assuming that your brother is as deserving of merit as you say, I would think he will be here shortly, apologizing for his lateness. Scientists have a great respect for numbers, and numbers are certainly involved in the telling of time."

"Yes." She glanced at the package still wrapped tightly in her arms. "I suppose I should leave this here. Please tell him this is the equipment he requires."

"Certainly," he said. "Fergus, take that from Miss Thornton and put it in Mr. Thornton's berth."

"Aye, Cap'n." Fergus took the oddly shaped bundle.

"Be careful!" she cried.

"We don't make a habit of destroying packages," Rupert said.

"Nope," Fergus said cheerfully and hauled the package away.

The woman's steely gaze remained fixed on him, as if assessing the likelihood that Fergus might buckle under the meager weight. "The contents are of the utmost importance."

"I assure you they will be safe," Rupert said.

He sighed. He would be happy when the ship set sail again. It was rare to find a woman so devoid of charm.

Chapter Four

The captain might not have been the first attractive man Louisa had met, but he certainly ranked as the most irritating.

This would be easier if he were a proper sea captain, the kind with gray whiskers and a face reddened more from decades of drink than delight at the sun.

Sea captains weren't supposed to look like Mediterranean deities reclining in gilded frames at the Royal Academy.

"Have you been to the West Indies before?"

"Naturally." The captain narrowed the distance between them.

If she'd thought his face distracting, it was only because she hadn't been focusing on his chest.

Which was now very clearly before her.

She attempted to avoid wondering how he managed to convey the appearance of strength so entirely while being swathed in a woolen tailcoat. She pondered the width of his shoulders and his towering height.

She was tall for a woman and was accustomed to

looking directly at a man, and not tilting her head up, so that she might see him while taking in the heavens. She was on a mission and had no time for arrogant sea captains, no matter how much their azure eyes smoldered, or how elegantly they strode.

His blue eyes twinkled as if unabashed at the pleasure he found in tormenting her, and she averted her gaze. No point contemplating the sultry curve of his lips.

Her mother may possess a proclivity to attire her in ridiculously hued frocks in a perhaps mistaken effort to make her more noticeable, but she never tended to mind. Now, though, she shivered under the captain's scrutiny.

Lack of notice was never Louisa's problem. Her mother could clothe her in all the canary or carmine colors she desired, but it wouldn't bring callers to Louisa's door.

Louisa refused to contemplate the descriptions, mostly combinations of a derogatory adjective and the word bluestocking, men used, not guilty at the possibility she might overhear.

"Farewell," she announced.

His eyebrows, swooping dark arches, swept upward. Likely he decided when he left ladies and not the other way around.

"Farewell," the captain said, and she forced herself not to linger on the pleasing tone of his voice.

She hurried over the deck, maneuvering over the assortment of ropes and knobs that signified everything mysterious, everything masculine, everything that Louisa would never know.

Waves rustled the ship, but she maintained her posture and climbed down the ladder to the rowboat.

Rain dappled her dress, and she bit away the scowl that threatened to spread over her face. Where on earth was

Mr. Thornton? She wished Becky had not lied and called him her brother. She glanced at Becky's still face. Had the scientist been scared to board the ship as well?

She shook her head. A man eager to dive in the West Indies was unlikely to be frightened by any sailors, even of the pirate or ex-pirate variety. Likely he was simply late. More than one visitor to Brighton had complained of the clay in the Weald that trapped carriage wheels with a horrifying regularity. Mr. Thornton had said he would also attend the ball, and she would see him there.

At least the package was waiting for him, just as they had planned. Her mother certainly would have noticed if she'd tried to haul her diving helmet to the ball. She smiled.

Perhaps in a few months, she would be able to read about the great discoveries he made with the diving helmet.

The rowboat moved through the water, and some gray shadows, their forms familiar, swam beside the boat

What would it be like to observe the fish that flitted along the coasts of the islands? So little was known about them. The scientific interest of the island dwellers seemed limited to techniques for achieving high sugar yields, knowledge that they clearly had not yet mastered, given their propensity for raising sugar tariffs and musings on the benefits of conquering new islands.

No one seemed interested in observing and recording the new world underneath their crystal waters. Rumors of jewel-toned fish derived from sailors, and some broadsheets off-handedly mentioned fish more vibrant than any they'd seen in between their lamentations on the corruption rampant in the West Indies and the privateers that ferociously guarded each island against corsairs and other intrepid invaders.

She cherished each mention of marine life, but it was time for someone to make a scholarly study. If there really were novel fish there, she desired to learn about them. Their physical traits and behavior should be studied and recorded. Every ichthyologist should have access to knowledge of fish outside their locality.

After they disembarked, Louisa and Becky hurried over the Marine Parade, passing finely attired men and women who seemed to scoff at their speed, if the slight raising of their noses coupled with the distinct downward curving of their lips, were any indication. *No matter.*

Chapter Five

Gliding along with composed, indifferent expressions would have to be for another day. Louisa's mother had asked to speak with her, and Louisa did not want her to wait any longer. Mother was already upset Louisa hadn't found a fiancé, and she had no intention of adding a worry about her ability to tell time to her mother's already lengthy woes.

Louisa rushed into the townhouse her stepfather had rented and scampered past side tables and settees, chosen more for their ability to resist damaging puddles and kleptomaniac tenants than style. Only a crystal chandelier hung high from the tiled floor to indicate this was a finer establishment, worthy of its equally high fee.

She ascended the stairs before the butler might greet her. Somehow regality came more naturally to servants than to her, and she'd no desire for a lecture, enhanced by carefully timed sniffs, on the general inabilities of Americans and mother's anxiousness to see her.

A mirror hung in the corridor, making the already grand space appear even more expansive. Louisa's thin frame seemed even more stick-like, swallowed by her billowing dress, and topped with frizzy locks. *Fiddle-faddle.* She smoothed her hair frantically.

After inhaling a large breath of the potpourri filled air, she approached her mother's door, braced herself for any possible barrage of admonishments and knocked. "Mama?"

Baritone and soprano murmurs sounded inside, and her chest tightened. Her stepfather must be home.

"Come in, darling!" Her mother's voice rang out.

Louisa stepped into the room and forced her lips to jut upwards. A thick smell of lavender and roses pervaded the chamber. Ample amounts of pastel colored pillows piled over the bed and seats, and cheery embroidered quotes with neatly stitched flowers dangled from the picture rail.

Her mother reclined on a fainting couch, attired in a silk robe containing such a collection of clashing colors that it would not have looked out of place if it were used as wallpaper at the Marine Pavilion. A deep rose stained her mother's cheeks, even though her mother never had a proclivity for rouge-applying accidents.

Her stepfather bent his torso in a practiced flourish, and Louisa dipped down into a rather less imperial curtsy.

"How do you do, Miss Carmichael?" He asked in the silky tone that all the women in society admired.

"Well," Louisa replied. "And you, Captain Daventry?"

"I always do well, Miss Carmichael," he said breezily. "When one works to having a good life, that's all one ever does."

"How...splendid," she chirped, and her gaze darted to her mother, who was gazing at him with open admiration.

Her chest tightened. She'd still not grown entirely accustomed to the captain, even though he was now her stepfather. She certainly had not grown accustomed to the dewy gazes her mother shot him with revolting frequency. She did not begrudge her mother a new husband after Louisa's father's death, but try as she might, she could not recall her mother ever gazing at her father in a similar manner. Was she in possession of a similar flaw, one that left men similarly indifferent toward her?

The captain's eyes flickered once again to her mother, and he smiled. "I will leave you two alone."

He departed through the adjoining door into his chambers. The townhouse might be large, but the walls did not mask the sound of the man singing to himself.

"Is he not so charming?" Her mother tied her robe more tightly. "You must take a sea captain as a lover at some point. After you're married of course," her mother said quickly, perhaps seeing something like shock in Louisa's expression. "Otherwise it would be most inappropriate."

"I suppose I should also wait until I procure the necessary heir and spares too?" Louisa asked.

Her mother beamed. "Yes, darling. You understand perfectly. I'm so pleased. Now do sit down."

Since her mother was taking up the entire fainting couch, as if practicing to be painted as a robed Venus, Louisa sat gingerly on the bed. The bedspread was more rumpled than well-trained chamber maids tended to leave for mothers of dukes, and Louisa gave her mother an uneasy smile.

"My darling daughter," her mother exclaimed. "I have news for you. You will not have to do another season!"

"Oh!" This time conjuring a smile took no effort, and pleasure swept through her with all the force of a wave.

Her mother must have understood that she desired to return to America. "That's wonderful."

Her mother nodded triumphantly. "Don't think I didn't know you were dreading it. A mother notices these things."

"I'm so pleased." Louisa beamed. "Thank you so much!"

Her mother's smile broadened. "Sometimes it just takes some motherly attention. But your life is set now, I promise. I didn't want to tell you before. I was hoping I could take care of everything, but I didn't want to get your hopes up."

Louisa sighed, conscious she must appear ridiculously content. The news was wonderful. Better than she'd ever dreamed of asking for. She could return to Massachusetts. She might continue her research. She wouldn't be forced to some unknown, landlocked region in England.

It would all be fine. Marvelous, in fact.

"I have found you a husband," her mother said brightly.

"Excuse me?" Louisa stammered, feeling the happiness vanishing, as if being pulled back with a low tide.

"You're to be married!" Her mother clapped her hands, and her bracelets, presents from India, jangled as the silver collided.

The news was nonsense. Louisa couldn't be engaged. She just couldn't be.

"To whom?" She stammered.

Her mother frowned and waved a hand loftily in the air. "Does it matter? But I assure you he's perfect. The son of a baronet. Not nobility of course, but at least he is the older son and will be bequeathed with property when his father passes." Her mother leaned closer to her in a conspiratorial fashion. "His father has expressed a great fondness for gorging on geese, so it might not be a long wait."

"Mother!"

Her mother settled back against the pile of luscious pillows. "Such considerations are important, my dear. You might not desire to admit it, but some of us live in a world not purely inhabited by sea creatures. He's even acquainted with your brother, Percival!"

"Oh." Louisa's shoulders relaxed somewhat.

"You'll meet him tonight."

"At the regent's ball?" Louisa strode toward her mother's bay window. A sliver of ocean stretched appealingly under the setting sun. Shards of pink and orange danced on the edge of the horizon, lighting the gray sky. "And this is the first I hear of it?"

"I didn't want you to be disappointed," her mother said gently. "I know how hard it's been lately. I'm sorry I wasn't more understanding. Please forgive me."

Louisa was silent, and her mother continued hastily, her voice shaking, as if eager to not dwell on her daughter's disapproval.

"It's really quite simple. And wonderful. Naturally. Well...a few days ago I received a letter from Sir Seymour Amberly, a baronet in Yorkshire. Apparently he read about you in *Matchmaking for Wallflowers* and decided you might be perfect for his son."

"He read about me?"

Her mother sighed. "I am afraid that you have become rather famous. I was sparing you the torment. I thought you might discover it on your own, but it seems you do not read women's magazines with enthusiasm. Here is the article."

Louisa's mother shoved a piece of paper toward her, and Louisa's stomach tightened uncomfortably. She picked up the paper:

Matchmaking for Wallflowers
Summer 1817
The Disastrous Debutante

Mrs. Daventry, new wife of the Massachusetts magnate, we weep with you.

No sorrow can be as great as that of a mother whose daughter has failed to impress the gentlemen of the ton. Your son may have inherited a dukedom, but our Englishmen rightfully dismissed your daughter as a disastrous debutante.

These pages cannot recall a woman who arrived in London with more advantages than Miss Louisa Carmichael. Sisters of handsome, heroic dukes are presumed to possess a modicum of charm and capabilities, and not speak in that consistently contemptible ex-colonial dialect, no matter which side of the world they were born.

We cannot blame Miss Carmichael's lack of a husband on her mother's lack of enthusiasm. No woman has accepted invitations at a more rapid pace than Mrs. Daventry.

Miss Carmichael may possess some advantages, but no man desires a wife who expounds upon the classification of fish with the enthusiasm with which she should be tackling dinner menus. Have hope, English roses. You can rise to great heights on the merit of your vigorous study of the rules of the ton and the whims of your suitors.

And whatever you do... Please leave discussions of fish to the fishermen.

— Your All Seeing, All Knowing, Always Anonymous Editor in Chief

Louisa's heartbeat thudded, and she pushed the paper away from her. How many people had read this?

"I was not aware that baronets read pamphlets targeted to debutantes," she said finally.

Her mother waved her hand dismissively. "Oh, everyone reads it. This is England. What else does its high society have to do except ridicule the behavior of their betters? It's not as if they are permitted to work! With the exception of the House of Lords of course, though I'm not convinced they do much of anything there. And too many of them rely entirely on their estate managers to run their property and wonder how they find themselves in dire straits. One really must give estate managers more guidance than telling them not to change anything." She smiled. "Mr. Daventry, of course, is much more accomplished."

Louisa returned her mother's smile. Even if she'd never yet managed to have a proper conversation with her stepfather, at least she could respect him. The man had made money as a sea captain, and though he was now wealthy, he lacked the bland propriety of aristocrats. Perhaps mother wouldn't have married him if she'd known Percival would become a duke. Louisa was glad she hadn't known: the captain seemed to make her mother content.

If only her mother would wait until Louisa met a man who promised to make her similarly happy.

"So this baronet was taken by the writer's description of me?" Louisa asked, conscious of the suspicious note in her voice.

"No, no, no. I believe actually it was the fact that you are Percival's sister. But your husband-to-be seems quite kind. And quite happy to be shown around Brighton by that nice young footman with the angelic curls. I do so like a man who is not bound too much by class rules. Almost American of him."

Louisa picked up one of her mother's pillows. She brushed her fingers over the embroidered fabric, noting how the sumptuous design still managed to be rough beneath her fingers. "I refuse to marry a stranger."

"How very dramatic of you," her mother said drily. "No need to fret though. He won't be a stranger for long, and there will be no need to delay the match. Sir Seymour assures me that he is the most powerful aristocrat in all Yorkshire. And you're to be married to his son!"

"So this person is not elderly?"

"He's on the right side of thirty-five."

Louisa frowned. "Right side for me? Or right side for you?"

"I will not have you reference my age," her mother said. "I have sacrificed my time to find you a husband, so you won't need to stress—"

"I know." Louisa's chest tightened. All the world knew about how Mr. Daventry had swept away her mother, even though unmarried men tended to go for younger women, and not widows with four children. Everyone knew that the captain was swarthy and mysterious with many tales of traveling to entertain everyone he met. Everyone declared it a travesty that her mother could not enjoy her new life with her new husband because she still had two unmarried daughters at home, and one new unmarried stepdaughter. And everyone knew that Louisa had not helped matters by not finding a husband.

"Anyway." Her mother moved to her dressing table and fluffed her already beautifully arranged hair. "He's on the right side of thirty-five if approaching his birthday."

Her eyes gleamed. "Not that it will matter. If he's anything like your stepfather, he'll be quite happy to fulfill his marital duties."

Louisa knew she had not eaten anything in hours, but her stomach constricted, as if she'd managed to swallow a bad shellfish.

"You are pale, my dear." Her mother's perfect skin creased. "I expected you to express more gratitude. You've begged me for so long to not do another season."

"I had hoped I might stay in Massachusetts..."

Where there is an ocean. Where there are lakes. Where I might conduct my research.

"Well, you imagined wrong. Your marriage will help your father and me. You mustn't expect us to keep you here indefinitely. Your father is very kind for hosting your new relatives."

"He's my stepfather," Louisa corrected.

Her mother shrugged. "Is precision so important? Finickiness is not a trait to be cultivated. You would have married long ago if not for your habit of correcting men. As if anyone is interested in your opinions of fish. The only useful pondering is which sauce is best to slather them in, and even that conversation is risky, lest your hostess's cook be planning them in one of your less favored ways."

Louisa attempted to contemplate a life too far from the ocean to avail herself of the scent of saltwater and ambles along the seashell-strewn shore, but her chest hurt.

"Perhaps he won't ask to marry me," Louisa said, more for her benefit than her mother's.

Something like disappointment flickered over her mother's face, but then she shook her head. "He endured a week-long journey to ask for your hand. If he can do that, he can make the short distance to the floor when he proposes."

"But he hasn't met me," Louisa said weakly.

"You are the sister of a duke."

"The sister of an unexpected duke," Louisa corrected.

Her mother waved a hand. "Niceties, only. No one will remember that in ten years."

"Which is tragic for our cousin who *died* at Waterloo."

Her mother's face sobered for a moment. "Let's not dwell on the past, darling. You're always telling us to look toward the future."

"That was about lauding science. Not about you secretly finding me a husband."

Her mother shrugged. "Not so secret. I'm telling you. One of my friends didn't tell her daughter that she was getting married until she was at the wedding."

"And when you say *friend*, you don't happen to mean yourself?" Louisa asked carefully. She couldn't be certain with her mother. She couldn't be certain about anything.

Not after her brother had found himself Duke of Alfriston, and not after her mother had gleefully packed them off to England to become aristocrats.

Her brother Percival might be a duke, but everyone knew it was because their cousin had died at Waterloo. Everyone knew their father had been the younger, unbeloved son who'd left England. Everyone knew their father had died and that Louisa's stepfather was as far from the *ton* as it was possible to be—he was an American, and not only a merchant but one who displayed a distinct pride in imports and exports.

The *ton* in London was all too clear to point out that it was simply a tragedy that the person groomed to become a duke had fallen in Waterloo. They mourned that a man of such good breeding could be replaced by a man with *American* sisters and a mother who'd spent the last twenty years living in Massachusetts, the very colony that had rewarded centuries of careful management with attacking the scarlet-uniformed soldiers who defended them. At least Percival had maintained his English accent.

The *ton* had shown suspicion toward Louisa, and she doubted Irene and Veronique would receive better receptions.

Especially not Veronique.

Her mother continued to bustle about. "What kind of wedding would it be if I had to keep it secret from everyone? I'm so thankful you've at least ceased spewing such nonsense about oceans. Who cares what fish might be there? They can't be very interesting—otherwise the good Lord wouldn't have put them where we couldn't see them."

"It would be misguided to characterize marine biology as nonsense," Louisa said carefully. The less her mother knew about her continued devotion to the subject, the better. "I was under the impression that I would return to London for a second season."

"And you've been complaining incessantly about it," her mother said. "Now you don't have to. And no one will be able to question why you didn't find a fiancé during your first season. You'll be quite respectable!"

"But—"

"Obviously you'll still attend balls in the future, but you won't have to be a wallflower."

"Who says I would be a wallflower?"

Her mother widened her eyes and laughed. The captain had referred to her mother's laughter as seraphic, but there seemed nothing heavenly about the sound to

Louisa. "Darling," her mother continued, "I would love to possess your confidence, but we both know..."

Louisa sighed.

"I mean..." her mother continued, "...I've tried to teach you. And your governesses have tried to teach you. But you weren't exactly a good student."

Louisa's smile tightened.

She was a good student. She was a good student in everything. Everything except what mattered to her mother and the rest of society.

She wasn't pretty enough, a fact that her mother laid entirely on her, even though, surely her mother's facial features and her father's facial features must be somewhat to blame. Though the English seemed fascinated with everything to do with the Romans and Greeks, they seemed less inclined to favor their downward turned noses, no matter how many porcelain statues they perched on their coffee tables and their bookcases, filled with doubtlessly unread books which displayed that very same characteristic.

Her hair didn't glisten like angels' feathers, and her gray eyes could neither be compared to verdant meadows nor cerulean skies.

She knew a lot, but the simple questions and small talk other people occupied themselves with bored her.

She rubbed a lock between her fingers, noting the slight coarseness, and the medium thickness. Normally her mother would criticize her and remind her that if young ladies paid too much interest to their hair, gentlemen might think they'd hidden an actual rat there.

This time her mother just gave her a bland smile. "Naturally I would not want to force you. But I truly do think it is the best option for you. You can't postpone the inevitable."

"I'll..." Louisa hesitated, but then said, "I'll meet him."

"Thank you."

She was getting married. And moving from the ocean. And though she could say no, though she could refuse to leave, she wasn't sure that she would.

Because perhaps her mother was right. What else would she do?

"But—" Louisa's chest hurt, even though her chest never hurt. Even though she was very, very healthy from all her swimming and her propensity to ramble the coast.

"Yes, dear?" Her mother's face was innocent, but her eyes flickered with something that looked like guilt.

"I—I wish there were an ocean there," Louisa stuttered. Even though she was precise with her words, and had excelled at dictation and debate—at least when her governesses had still deigned to teach her that, before they concentrated solely on flower arrangements and French conversations.

"Perhaps you're too old for the ocean," her mother said. "We can't be young forever."

"But the ocean is everything." The sentence felt like an understatement. The ocean was big and expansive and so beautiful. The sea could vary so easily, and Louisa never, ever tired of looking at it. Or swimming in it. And observing everything that lived there.

"Harrogate is tolerable. If you insist on reading those dreadfully dull tomes, you won't even notice the lack of good company. Though your sister-in-law's family lives there, so you shouldn't feel too abandoned. In fact Sir Seymour's son, Cecil Amberly is Fiona's cousin."

"Oh." She smiled. She did like Fiona. Surely Fiona's

cousin couldn't be so very dreadful, even if it did seem odd that neither Fiona nor Percival had mentioned him when she'd visited Harrogate last spring.

"That's all very enlightening," she said quickly. "I'll—er—ponder it."

"See that you do." Her mother's face brightened, likely sensing that Louisa was not going to quarrel with her, at least not now.

"And if I do not like—"

"Louisa, I hope you do not mean to suggest *not* marrying him. You had your chance this whole season. You met every eligible man in Great Britain. No one deemed you suitable for them—how on earth do you expect that you have the luxury to select your own match?"

Louisa sighed. She would never find a better match, and she wouldn't be permitted to stay at home. She knew it. Everyone knew it.

Louisa pressed her lips together. She would argue. She promised herself she would argue.

But it was difficult to do that when her mother was correct. She'd been given every luxury. And she'd tried—honestly, she'd tried. She'd danced frequently, laughed at the young men's attempts at wit, and allowed herself to be squeezed into the gowns her mother deemed suitable.

But though the men may have enjoyed the thought of having a duke as a brother-in-law, all of them seemed to find superior satisfaction in the English debutantes scattered at every ball who could be trusted with not introducing irregular flatware arrangements for the household staff.

And perhaps...perhaps also her conversation hadn't

helped. Perhaps when the men inquired on the pleasantness of the journey across the Atlantic, they hadn't really intended to receive a categorization of the number and type of whales and dolphins she'd seen.

Despite her best attempts, she'd failed at finding a husband herself. Her failure did not earn her the right to live a life as a bluestocking, ensconced in a cozy cottage with tomes of leather-bound books displaying fish. She couldn't expect her mother and stepfather to take care of her forever.

Her mother gazed at her, and for a moment Louisa imagined her mother might express some sentiment of regret. Instead her mother flickered her hand. "Prepare yourself."

For what? A ball or a lifetime of misery?

Chapter Six

Mr. Thornton, despite his supposed success at science and his presumable understanding of how to read a clock, had still not appeared.

"Bloody passengers," Fergus scoffed. "Don't reckon we should 'ave gotten one. Ain't right to 'ave a man on board who ain't gonna be pillaging along with us and ain't gonna be working."

"Working is *all* you'll do," Rupert reminded him. "We've been over this. We're respectable."

"You may 'ave picked up a fancy accent from your high and mighty captains when you were a cabin boy to 'em, but we both know you ain't fancy." Fergus winked. "They don't be dragging off the children of gentry and aristocrats to join the Royal Navy. Good workin' stock," he said cheerfully. "That's what we are."

Fergus grinned into the horizon, and even though the man's smile tended to be contagious, and even though Rupert's strength was frequently remarked on, the effort of pulling his lips into a similar smile seemed impossible to achieve.

I should have told him.

I should tell him now.

He shook his head. Some secrets were too large to share. His men respected him for being one of them. When they saw him, they wanted to be him one day. Perhaps Fergus had no aspirations to captain his own ship, but some of the sailors did. How could he tell them that his birth, his education had allowed him to leap into the pirate role, even though that was the very position that should be most open to people of less vaunted births?

He didn't want people to gossip about the ship, about his birth. He didn't desire to find his hull bursting with crates from merchants who simply wanted to impress his father.

There was a way that would relieve the crew's apprehension.

He shook his head.

Perhaps he was giving up being a pirate, but he certainly wouldn't abandon every instinct for privacy. He'd worked too hard to maintain his anonymity. He wasn't going to stop that now. Not with his father still alive. Not when he might be dragged to handle some estate and pretend to not notice his father's boorish behavior.

Not that his parents desired anything to do with him.

No. He shook his head.

Some things were best kept secret.

"Any income is good," Rupert said solemnly, and his lips twitched. "Especially since he's already paid. If he doesn't show up, all the better."

"Aye." Then his face became more pensive, and Fergus thrummed a finger over his chin, as if still expecting to find the bushy red beard he'd sported to be there. "It's just piracy did 'ave a bigger income."

Rupert smiled. Fergus was just nervous that he could no longer run his fingers through French jewels to physically ascertain their wealth.

"I would think you would be at least somewhat relieved to have the prospect of a violent death lessened," Rupert said.

Fergus shrugged.

"And you always have the option of leaving. You no longer need to honor your pirate vow."

Fergus widened his eyes. "And leave you, Cap'n? I would sooner—"

"Have a passenger on board?" Rupert asked.

Fergus's cheeks darkened.

"I'm going out." Rupert declared and then lowered one of the smaller boats.

"'Bout time, Cap'n," Fergus said, recovering. "Reckon you'll enjoy being back on good old English soil."

Rupert grunted. Enjoy wasn't the proper word.

Despise, hate, abhor came closer to the emotions he was anticipating feeling.

He was being unfair.

He was looking forward to his meeting tonight. But he was all too aware he could be disappointed. It could be a trap.

Never mind.

A few enthusiastic swimmers still splashed in the sea, and Rupert gazed at them almost wistfully. There'd been a time when he might have joined them.

Those days were long past.

Swimming was an occupation for other people, ones with different memories.

The sky was white and devoid of texture from clouds as if all focus should be on the coastal town. Perhaps the regent had bribed some heavenly body. Cordelia had mentioned the prince was holding a ball tonight, and the man certainly spent money on everything else.

Further inland there would be valleys and well-maintained fields, but only the slight curve of cliffs at the edge of the town hinted at the countryside.

Rupert hadn't thought he would miss the sculptured hedges, groomed by centuries of gardeners, that looped around his father's estate.

My estate.

He pushed that thought away. The estate was miles away. He wasn't here to visit his parents. His father's behavior had assured that.

Soon he would be back at sea, where he belonged.

He couldn't let word of his aristocracy get back to his crew.

And he certainly couldn't let word get out to the people he worked for—he wanted to succeed on his own merits, and not on a title gained by a father who occupied himself with lending money to aristocrats and then sending henchmen after them when they could not pay the vast interest rates.

He climbed down the ladder, and one of his sailors rowed him to the shore, moving the oars easily through the still water.

His legs wobbled. It had been too long since he'd been on firm land. He moved his gaze to the rows of new buildings and pulled the brim of his hat further down.

It wouldn't do for anyone to recognize him.

He felt safe from the merchants who put their wares on *The Sapphire Princess.* But this street was different.

He wrapped his arms together. Perhaps he was a fool to meet with her. Perhaps he wouldn't find her at all. Perhaps he'd only find his father and experience a barrage of words as his father chided him for not desiring to have anything to do with his family.

But if there was a chance it was actually his sister, he would bloody well take it.

The street was empty, and Rupert grinned. It could not be more evident that the regent was having a ball. The *ton* tended to complain about the royal family, mocking the royals' valiant attempts to squeeze into the latest fashions, despite their decidedly stocky German figures, as well as their even feebler grasp of warfare and world politics.

Yet whenever a ball was held, the regent could not find himself alone, no matter how much his outrageous behavior appeared in the broadsheets and gossip papers. The man's position had only been elevated since Rupert had last been in England, despite the multitudes of scandals that clung to him. The regent's glee at destroying buildings in the center of London to put up boulevards leading to an even costlier palace for himself, seemed to be forgiven, just as his brazen adulteries and outrageous lies placing himself as a hero in a war he'd never fought in.

Rupert would not complain that the street was quiet. He sauntered up the marble steps to Cordelia's townhouse, gave the lion knocker a hard thud against the door, and waited for his fate.

A servant swung open the door, and Rupert stepped inside the townhouse. He swung his gaze around the room, half-expecting his father.

Instead a high-pitched voice shrieked his name.

He blinked, and in the next moment a woman ran toward him, her blonde hair bouncing against her back. A broad-shouldered man with twinkling eyes soon followed her.

"Rupert!" The woman exclaimed.

"Cordelia?"

It was his sister.

His lovely sister.

Whom he hadn't seen since she was a child.

"You're older!" The words lacked the articulateness that he prided, but his sister merely smiled. She wrapped her arms around him, and this time he didn't need to bend down to reach her or to lift her in his arms.

She was a woman.

A married woman. With a husband right beside her.

"Lord Metcalfe." The man bowed, and Rupert noted the Scottish brogue.

He smiled. He'd never expected his sister to marry a Scot. He echoed the man's bow. "Lord Rockport."

"I thought you had died," Cordelia said, her voice mournful. His heart squeezed.

"I wouldn't do that," he said, forcing his tone to be light, but for a moment he thought of all those times he'd come so close to doing just that.

War was brutal.

"Come inside," Lord Rockport said, smiling.

Rupert followed them into the townhouse, stepping over the black and white tiled floor. Candelabras illuminated the elaborate emerald green wallpaper and shadows flickered over the gilded chairs and sideboards.

"Do you own this place?" Rupert asked.

"We're just renting it for the week," Lord Rockport said.

"We spend most of our time in Scotland," Cordelia said.

It wasn't what he would have expected of her. He would have thought his sister would display the rigid mannerisms of the ladies of the *ton* he knew. The mannerisms of their mother.

But instead she seemed happy and joyful.

"I do wish you were staying longer," Cordelia murmured.

He settled into a seat.

Cordelia's face sobered. "Father would like to see you."

"So that he might chain me to the estate?" Rupert scoffed. "I am perfectly content."

"That's good." She hesitated. "And I understand if you don't want to see him again, but I should tell you that he is unwell. You may not have another chance."

Oh.

Rupert's heart sank. Death was always tragic. He knew that, even though he'd bestowed it on many people when battling on behalf of the crown. He'd never taken somebody's life without considering the hopes and dreams he was slicing away.

He didn't want his father to die. But could he rush to his bedside, delaying his ship, and giving up the life he'd worked to achieve? Could he trust his father to keep his presence secret? And would his meeting with his father—a man who'd always prided himself on being unpleasant and vengeful to others, achieve anything?

"Perhaps I'll visit when I return," he said.

Cordelia nodded. "I understand."

"The man likes his adventures," Lord Rockport said. "But next time stay for longer."

"I hope you didn't travel down from Scotland just for my benefit." He shuddered at the thought of the long journey.

"We would have come down anyway," Cordelia said.

"Though as it happens we were hoping to spend some time with some of our friends."

"Ah..." Rupert nodded.

"I wish you could meet them," Cordelia said. "There's one woman who is quite fascinated with the sea—"

"Please," Rupert said. "Do not attempt to matchmake me. I'm perfectly content."

Lord Rockport chuckled. "I was you once. Let's speak of other things then."

"Yes! There's so much to learn," Cordelia exclaimed.

A strange warmth filled Rupert. He wasn't used to being away from his ship, away from his crew. He'd spent so many years decrying England, thinking of all his father represented, but for the first time, he wondered if he'd been unjust.

He rather wished he wasn't sailing to the West Indies tomorrow morning.

*

Rain continued to splatter upon the Indian domes and minarets of the Marine Pavilion, though none of the guests seemed particularly worried at the possible destruction of their carefully chosen attire. Debutantes strolled triumphantly inside, grasping onto the arms of their fawning fiancés more from an urge to brandish them than from worry of falling.

"Don't dilly-dally," her mother exclaimed, and Louisa scrambled down the slippery steps of the coach.

Some debutantes, women with whom she'd chatted at the start of the season, when they'd both been equally hopeful and intimidated, flashed her smug looks.

They've read the article.

Louisa held her head in the most regal manner she could emulate and attempted to brush past them.

"Oh, you are eager to meet Mr. Amberly," her mother said.

Louisa attempted to smile, conscious of more gazes directed at them.

Ignoring the other debutantes would be more feasible if the entrance were not quite so crowded. No matter how much everyone delighted in laughing at the architecture of the Marine Pavilion, happy to assert their tastes as superior to that of a royal, no one declined an invitation.

"Is that—?"

"From the article?"

"The fish girl?"

Louisa stiffened. They were speaking about her. Right before her. As if the fact that they were not referring to her by name meant that the several feet between them were nonexistent.

She directed her steeliest gaze at them. "I always believed speaking about other people was frowned upon. But if that's not the case—I'm sure there are plenty of things I could say about you."

She couldn't actually, but their faces still whitened, and they murmured quick apologies and pushed further into the throng.

She sighed. She despised whoever had decided to sell her struggles as entertainment. Her mother was correct. The faint hope she'd clung to that she might find a fiancé had dissipated after the article. No one would want to be associated with her now.

No one except this Cecil Amberly.

Unease prickled through her. It truly was most odd that Percival had not invited her to meet Sir Seymour and his family when she'd visited Harrogate earlier in the year. Could this man truly be as wonderful as her mother claimed?

She sighed. *Likely not.*

At least she had the meeting with Mr. Thornton to look forward to.

Next year at this time she would be reading the articles that he'd published from his scientific research. Perhaps, if she were very lucky, she might even provide assistance. Some scientists expressed distaste for formatting citations correctly, and perhaps he might condescend to allow her to help.

She smiled and followed her mother inside the palace.

Sumptuous art, seemingly chosen more for their disparity to anything English than their quality, hung from the walls, and competed with flamboyantly patterned wallpaper.

Despite the lack of carriages grinding over gravel and the dearth of prancing horses, the inside of the palace exceeded even the outside in noise. Women wearing feathered headpieces jostled beside their top-hat-adorned husbands. Other young ladies wore demure pastel and ivory gowns. Only the occasional scalloped hem or chevron-striped sleeves differentiated them.

Louisa knew better than to linger. She scurried past them, not caring if they thought her impolite.

"I'll meet you inside," she called to her mother, once she'd managed to weave up some of the stairs. Skinniness held some advantages.

She wove through the heavily perfumed *ton*.

Everyone laughed merrily, murmuring over when the regent might make an appearance.

Louisa was not interested in when the regent might

decide he'd been sufficiently fed to greet the guests lofty enough to be in his ballroom, though not of sufficient appeal to share his food. There was another person she would far rather see.

Likely she would notice Mr. Thornton at once, would be able to spot his regal brow and appealing sensitive nature. A man who cared about fish and dolphins would be sensitive.

And of course, this man *dove*. He would be athletic—not like the tubby older men eager to regale guests on made-up adventures overseas.

Her smile widened, and she changed into her dance slippers.

Her dress might reflect more her mother's taste than the dictates of current fashion, but for the first time she did not worry at all that others might find the vibrant blue garish.

Mr. Thornton would not be concerned with her appearance. His mind would be lofty, drawn to important discussions like any man of ideas.

She entered the ballroom, conscious of her gown swishing against the finely dressed guests. Her shawl dangled from her shoulders, though now, under the gaze of the *ton*, she would be happier if it covered her entirely. She opened her fan in an attempt to resemble some form of demureness.

Men in glossy ebony tailcoats chatted to one another, clutching crystal tumblers in their hands. She smiled, remembering when she'd once cared whether one of these men might offer to dance with her. She wasn't searching for some young aristocrat, she was searching for someone far finer—a distinguished academic. She brushed past the silk-clad women, attired in colors favorable to their complexions, and craned her neck around the ballroom to see if she could spot a man of the professional luster worthy of a man in possession of the scholar's vast qualities and sublime curriculum vitae.

"My dear!" Her mother's voice barreled toward her.

Louisa cringed and swiveled around.

Her mother rushed toward her, nearly tumbling over the undoubtedly recently polished floor. She straightened her turban, so the ebony feathers pointed triumphantly upward. "You must meet your future husband! The love of your life! The father of your children!"

"I—"

"They're up in Heaven now, anxious to be born! You must meet him. You cannot tarry a second!"

Louisa blinked.

"Come on." Her mother dragged her through the swarm of people, bumping against the guests' glossy attire. The violinists' upbeat music swallowed Louisa's hurried apologies, and she had the distinct, uncomfortable sensation that somebody had splattered brandy over her dress.

Dashing through a crowded room filled with people eagerly sipping drinks was unideal.

Finally her mother halted.

"Behave," her mother whispered, continuing to grip her wrist, as if wary of Louisa fleeing.

This is him.

"Is that Miss Carmichael?" An English accent sounded, and the stern baritone voice prickled her spine.

Louisa swung around to meet her fate.

Perhaps he was on the right side of thirty-five, but if so, the English must age most terribly. His figure was expansive, as if he'd decided to attain a gravitas by sheer consumption of food rather than deeds.

"Mr. Amberly?" Louisa dipped into a curtsy, though his eyes seemed more intent on assessing her technique than welcoming her. Too late she remembered that she should wait to be introduced to him before addressing him. Mother would scold her later. Americans might be forward, but not Englishwomen. And certainly not aristocratic Englishwomen.

Bushy eyebrows scrunched together beneath a white wig, and his face seemed to strive to match his puce waistcoat.

"I am not Mr. Amberly," he said. "I am Sir Seymour Amberly. The *baronet*."

"Your fiancé is there." Her mother pointed to a large man wearing a lilac tailcoat. No gray streaked his hair, and a surge of relief swept through Louisa.

Just a very *small* surge.

She still did not desire to be married, and his appearance did not compel her to abandon all her dreams.

"I am your new father," Sir Seymour announced.

She frowned. She had a father—in Heaven.

The baronet narrowed the distance between them, and his dark eyes continued to scrutinize her. "Her hair is too thick. Look, she can barely tie it back. Most disgraceful."

She stiffened, and her heartbeat leaped inside her chest, as if desiring to escape from the man's unapologetic rudeness.

A group of finely dressed women directed their gazes toward her, not bothering to cover their smirks. Even their musings on the Marine Pavilion's décor could not occupy them completely in the presence of such boorishness.

"I know she might not appear much," her mother said

carefully, and Louisa despised the sudden nervous expression on her mother's face.

"Ha!" Sir Seymour uttered a harsh laugh and adjusted his quizzing glass. He scrutinized her, his gaze coursing over her body with the expertise of a man prone to evaluating every woman he happened upon.

Finally he sighed heavily and slipped his quizzing glass into his pocket as if he'd resigned himself to not having any pleasant feelings after thinking of her.

"Her hips are narrow," Sir Seymour remarked. "Rather mannish. Are you certain she's up to having children?"

"I had four," her mother said affronted.

"Well, that's good." Sir Seymour paused and then rolled his gaze over her mother. "But then, you, my dear, do not lack for curves. What a bosom!"

Her mother paused but then gave an awkward giggle that Louisa had not known her capable of.

Everyone knew about her mother's charms. The captain had proposed to her before all of Boston's high society, lauding her beauty with such enthusiasm that a Boston paper had chosen to print his proposal, forever immortalizing her mother's charms.

Some whispered that it was unfortunate that her father had not been in possession of an equal degree of handsomeness to guarantee the bequeathal of beauty to his children. Lamentations from the more gossip-prone members of society that the captain was not her father and that she hadn't inherited his wide-set eyes and regal bearing had also not escaped her attention. Some people even declared it a waste that the captain had limited himself to one child, one he'd had with the wrong woman.

Her mother's cheeks remained pink, and she flashed

a tight, uncomfortable smile. "You are too kind, Sir Seymour."

"Indeed? I do not recollect witnessing any kindness," Louisa remarked.

Her mother's bright blue eyes widened with an alarming rapidity. "My dear!"

"Chit's got a temper," Sir Seymour mused, and some onlookers smirked.

Humiliation soared through her, but she clenched her fingers together.

"I don't like to think what my grandchildren will be like. Carrying the Amberly family traits is a most momentous task."

"She understands it," her mother said hastily. "And think how wonderful it will be if your dear child sires sons with her! Debate skills are in much demand. Why, I could see a grandchild of yours, with my daughter's assistance, reaching the very highest heights of the House of Lords. Perhaps he might even be a future prime minister!"

"No descendant of mine should tarnish his fingers by worrying about the problems of the lower orders," Sir Seymour declared, and Louisa's mother lower lip wobbled.

Louisa despised that her mother seemed so eager for the match. She hadn't realized what a burden she'd been.

"Still..." Sir Seymour's smile broadened. "Cecil *is* certain only to sire sons. He possesses my virility."

"Most obviously." Her mother nodded vigorously. She glanced into the crowd. "Now where is my dear husband? Ah, there he is."

Louisa had never been so happy to see her stepfather. He strode through the crowd, armed with two drinks and handed one to her and her mother. "Lemonade."

Her mother's smile wobbled, and Louisa had the

strangest sense that her mother would have favored something stronger.

Louisa took the drink eagerly, happy to occupy her hands, lest she do something more drastic with them—such as slap her future father-in-law.

"It would be useful to have a grandson who is not afraid to have words with the magistrate," Sir Seymour mused. "I've found that my local magistrate is most reluctant to try people for poaching. Such soft-heartedness! Just because poaching is a capital crime, the magistrate insists that no man is tried without being caught in the act. Better safe than sorry, that's what I always say!"

Sir Seymour shook his head, readjusting his wig when it toppled too much down one side.

"Perhaps it is wise to trust the magistrate's judgment," her mother said.

Louisa peered again through the throngs of smartly coiffed women and broad-shouldered Corinthians toward her future husband, the man who would be her closest companion.

In truth, it was odd Mr. Amberly hadn't displayed any curiosity in her, but then again, he did appear to be having an intent conversation with another gentleman, one wearing a lavender waistcoat. Perhaps they were remarking on the coincidence of their similar attire. That would explain why they kept brushing each other's shoulders.

Or perhaps—

Louisa frowned. Hadn't her mother mentioned that he'd spent the day with an attractive footman? That wasn't something members of the *ton* did willingly. She knew about certain men. Knew about their inclinations.

She was not utterly naive.

Perhaps she was mistaken.

And even if she wasn't, it wouldn't matter. She'd never expected romance.

But for some indescribable fashion, a lump still seemed to form in her throat.

Perhaps she hadn't expected romance, seeing that more as the future for the prettier members of the *ton:* the ones with violet eyes, delicate features, and silky blonde locks.

But hadn't she hoped for it? Longed for it as well? Even when reason told her such dreams were better suited for fairy tales and her sister's penny romances?

Louisa raised her fan and fluttered it over her face. Clearly some clever person had invented them for just this situation—hiding facial expressions from insufferable conversation partners.

"How are you enjoying Brighton?" Mr. Daventry asked.

"Ah...Brighton is tolerable." Sir Seymour's booming voice interrupted her thoughts. "So many foreigners though."

Her mother glanced nervously at her husband who had developed a stony expression on his face.

"I've heard they ship Frenchmen in regularly from Dieppe." Sir Seymour shook his head. "Disgraceful. As if there weren't a reason the good Lord created a channel to keep us from foreigners."

"I am one of these foreigners you speak of," Mr. Daventry drawled.

"How unfortunate. But no use dwelling on the matter," Sir Seymour said patiently.

Mr. Daventry glowered, and Louisa waited for Sir Seymour to grovel.

"Perhaps you should get yourself a drink," Louisa's mother said gently to the captain, and the man stomped back into the crowd in the direction of the punch table.

"At least we can avail ourselves of fine wine again." Louisa's mother smiled brightly.

Sir Seymour shrugged. "Never stopped getting that. That's what smuggling is for."

Louisa blinked. She might not have lived in England during the war, but she was certain smuggling had lacked legality.

"Bloody shame all those privateers, attacking all those ships bringing good French and Spanish products to our shores. Raising the prices, that's what they did. Most dreadful business."

Somehow the image of Captain Rosse invaded her mind. Her maid had been so frightened of the man's supposed pirating past. Still, she found herself frowning at Sir Seymour's continued tirade. "But didn't the Royal Navy pay them to do that? And forbid smuggling?"

"I'm sure they just meant to do that for the riff-raff. The plebeians and such. A baronet cannot be separated from his drink. It's just not proper."

"I see," Louisa said, even though that was the one thing she was struggling to do in Sir Seymour's presence.

"So many foreigners frown when they speak with me," Sir Seymour lamented. "I suppose it must be that my presence reminds them of the regret they feel at not being English."

"You are rather English," her mother said.

Sir Seymour beamed. "And you need not worry. Your

dear daughter will be most certainly taken care of. My wife and I will teach her to speak English."

"I do speak English!" Louisa exclaimed, but Sir Seymour held up his hand.

"Not that ex-colonial variety," he said.

"I would not consider American English improper—" Louisa protested, but her mother frowned, and she resisted the urge to argue.

"My son is greatly interested in culture. He is always in London and Paris and has many artistic friends. He was most saddened when Sir Mulbourne, that great art critic, died."

"What a caring nature he has," Louisa murmured.

"He has said that he was reluctant to marry earlier because of his great passion for art."

"A worthy pastime," Louisa said.

"Far better than...fish. Who was it who interested herself in that? Most absurd."

Her mother's face whitened.

Louisa lowered her fan.

It didn't matter if Sir Seymour saw the fury on her face. She didn't care.

This was her life.

If the Amberlys did not find her sufficiently suitable for their dear only child, she would not protest.

"*I* am interested in fish," Louisa said.

"What?" Sir Seymour frowned. "Ah... The article. Of course!"

His eyes twinkled, and she had the uncomfortable sensation that he may have attempted to rile her up.

Well, if so, he had succeeded.

"Marine life is fascinating," Louisa declared.

"How amusing." Sir Seymour's laugh barreled through

the room, and her mother's shoulders sagged. "I'm a meat man myself. Lambs, pheasants, I'm not impartial. If I can see the blood when I cut into it, all the better." He scrutinized her. "Do you not find it most distressing that you cannot see any blood when you cut into a fish on your plate? It makes the meal greatly decrease in amusement."

"Well, perhaps, if the fish were not cooked... And if you were to eat whale—"

"Hmm... Perhaps those fishermen have a point." He beamed. "You might be a good sort of daughter-in-law after all."

"G-good," she said. "Not that I would advocate eating whale."

Whales were very large. Their deaths would not be painless.

"Whales are for lamps, not food! You Americans. And they say *we've* got a mad king. Don't know what sort of leaders you lot have to fill your mind with such absurd thoughts." He smiled. "Tell you what, when you're in Yorkshire, I'll teach you to shoot."

"That won't be—"

He smiled. "Now I know what you're going to say. You're going to say that you couldn't possibly encroach on my time. That shooting requires an agility of mind and hand that you do not possess." He sighed. "And perhaps you don't. But I will still strive to teach you. Everyone should be able to shoot a living being. Can't say you're living if you don't."

Louisa frowned. She knew how to shoot. Not that she had any desire to do so with the baronet.

"I promise you now, even if you find that you are incapable of the sturdiness of soul to shoot, I will make sure that I will teach your sons—my grandchildren—how to do that. I'll make sure that they have a gun in the hand before they can walk."

Before?

"That won't be necessary," Louisa exclaimed, and Sir Seymour frowned.

Louisa's heart wobbled. "Perhaps it is time for me to meet Mr. Amberly?"

She hadn't thought herself desirous to meet him, but now she couldn't wait for something, anything, to distract her.

And she had the uncomfortable realization that she couldn't imagine raising children in the same home as Sir Seymour and his wife. He'd insulted her family and her too much.

"Cecil! Oh, Cecil!" Sir Seymour's voice thundered through the ballroom. "I have your wife for you."

Mr. Amberly trotted toward his father and nodded amiably. "Ah! Delighted to make your acquaintance."

"The pleasure is all mine," she stumbled automatically.

"I hope my father has been diverting," he said.

"I suppose he could be attributed with that quality."

"Splendid," Sir Seymour said and turned to his son. "I'm a bit worried about the size of her hips."

"Oh?" Mr. Amberly scrutinized them, and she realized that unlike his father, he'd hardly seemed interested in her at all. "Nothing wrong with them!"

"But she's hardly got a bosom," Sir Seymour said. "If I didn't know better, I might think her a man dressed in a gown. Most undignified."

Her cheeks burned. Her mother was beside her.

"Ah!" Mr. Amberly assessed her. "No, she looks all female to me."

"Hmm... Then you've got a keener eye than me," Sir Seymour said. "The boy's an expert!"

Mr. Amberly shrugged and turned to her. "Anyway, let's get the wedding over with soon. We better get those banns published. Unless the archbishop is here somewhere."

"Why don't we just pop up to London? Much more dignified." He glanced at this father. "And faster."

"So soon?" Louisa stammered. "You haven't even asked me."

Sir Seymour laughed loudly. "Better do that, boy! The lady needs a proposal."

"Right." Mr. Amberly seemed unsure of what to do.

"Perhaps you mean to invite her to the balcony?" Sir Seymour suggested and clapped his hand against Mr. Amberly's back.

"Exactly!" He beamed. "That's precisely what I meant to do!"

"Marvelous," she murmured.

Mr. Amberly headed in the direction of some curtains, and Louisa scrambled after him. She needed to get this over with. She still needed to speak with Mr. Thornton.

The room seemed filled with less distinguished types, and she sighed. She would find him later.

Mr. Amberly opened the door. "I suppose you better call me Cecil now. What with the marriage and everything."

The faint scent of roses and foxgloves from the garden could not lessen the unpleasant chill of the harsh evening breeze, and the giggles and moans of other couples could not distract her from the significance of this moment.

Her heart hadn't ceased squeezing at the mention of marriage, but she merely nodded. "My name is Louisa."

"I know." Cecil flourished his hand, gesturing for her to step onto the balcony.

"I see." The door closed behind her, and she gazed at her husband-to-be. He beamed back at her, as if expecting praise that he'd researched her Christian name.

This wasn't right.

This wasn't anything like the couples in Loretta Van Lochen's stories. And though she knew more than most people just how unrealistic and far-fetched those stories were, just how little the author herself knew, she still yearned for a modicum of romance.

She hadn't even found logic.

"And you still desire to marry me?" She didn't desire to continue. She had no desire to reflect on her humiliation at all. But she had to. "The article essentially said I was the woman in England least bestowed with popularity."

"Well..." Cecil shifted his legs over the stone balcony and squeezed the railing with his hand, seemingly unconscious that he might sully his ivory gloves. "The truth is..." He moved his hand over his elaborate, embroidered waistcoat and then ruffled his hand through his immaculate, perfect coiffure. He focused his gaze away from her, though she was certain he was not contemplating the shrubs. "The truth is, I don't much mind. Look. I've never met you before. And you've never met me. But you're still willing to marry me. After that article, I think you would be willing to marry anyone."

He laughed, though she did not join him.

"What I'm trying to say," he said, "is if you desire to marry for love, you shouldn't pick me." His voice firmed, and his eyes hardened. "Trust me."

She nodded. She understood what he wasn't saying.

He shrugged. "But I think the match will be good. My

parents are desirous of a match, and you have no one else to marry you. Your connections will gratify my parents, and I promise that I won't be around much."

Perhaps he had a point. He didn't seem...bad. In fact, he seemed rather nice.

"I'm not sure your father would be a good influence on our children," she said.

He smiled. "I doubt we'll have any. Not everyone does."

She blinked. "Oh."

Well.

That solved that issue.

Somewhat.

"So what do you say?" he asked. "Shall we make a go of it?"

Her heart still squeezed, but she couldn't think of an excuse.

Her mother was right. She'd failed her season.

If she only had some time...

The captain's face dashed through her mind, and she pushed away the image. Chiseled cheekbones, sturdy jaws and deep blue eyes had no right invading her mind.

"Well. I suppose you have no objections." Cecil glanced toward the ballroom. "I better get off to those chaps. It's not every day you're in a new town."

"I suppose that's true," Louisa said, startled. She followed him from the balcony.

"All settled," Cecil announced to Sir Seymour and her mother.

"Darling," her mother cried out and rushed toward her. Even Sir Seymour managed to smile.

Cecil gave a curt nod and then hurried toward his new friends.

Chapter Seven

Louisa had never associated her mother with strength, but after being hugged by her, she was reassessing her previous opinion.

Or perhaps she'd merely lost all her strength. Her legs wobbled, as if unable to hold the furious beating within her chest. Her blood seemed to thunder through her veins, as if willing her to escape.

What have I done?

"Well," her mother said. "I know you don't like balls, and it is getting late..."

Louisa straightened. They couldn't leave now. She still needed to find Mr. Thornton. This was her last chance before the ship left tomorrow morning, and she needed to explain how the diving helmet worked.

"Perhaps it's best if I mingle."

Her mother smiled and released her hold. "Of course. I'm sure you'll want to spread the news."

"Y-yes."

"You can hold your chin high now," her mother called after her.

Louisa smiled weakly and avoided the more curious gazes of onlookers. She pushed through the crowd.

Soon she would meet the scientist who would accomplish all her dreams.

Mr. Thornton would take her diving machine and make great discoveries while in the West Indies. She imagined taking his research and analyzing it, writing about it, publishing it.

She closed her eyes, imagining L. Carmichael cited in groundbreaking articles on the ocean.

It wouldn't be the first name cited, despite its distinct alphabetical advantage over Thornton.

In fact it probably wouldn't even be able to be published with her name on it, because honestly, she was a woman and she didn't want that fact to hamper the seriousness of the research or diving helmet.

But when she closed her eyes, when she daydreamed, her name was on the papers, anyway.

She clutched her reticule and scanned the ballroom for a man of distinguished and athletic appearance. She grabbed some lemonade from the banquet table and strove to amble authoritatively through the ballroom.

"I believe it is appropriate for me to suggest that the two of us dance." An older, portly man interrupted her quest.

"No, thank you." She craned her neck and attempted to spot Thornton.

The elderly gentleman raised his eyebrows. "I do not observe you dancing with anyone else."

"Forgive me," she apologized. Her wallflower status provided her with little excuses to not be in his company. Certainly no one else was offering to dance with her—not even her own fiancé.

"Perhaps later then," he said.

"I'm not sure..." For someone so old, he certainly was persistent. Evidently he'd had decades of practice at being frustrating.

"But you are Miss Carmichael, are you not?" He pushed a worn quizzing glass over his eye and peered at her.

"I—" She frowned. "Have we been introduced?"

"Well... That would be unwise. This is supposed to be secret," he said, readjusting his quizzing glass. "Remember?"

She chilled.

"You're most scrawny."

"Excuse me?" she stammered.

He shrugged his shoulders in a languid, lackadaisical manner. "Doesn't worry me. I was expecting it. A man can have dreams though, right?"

Her eyes widened. "Are you..."

He couldn't be.

He absolutely couldn't be the man that she'd corresponded with. The man who was supposed to do research in the Caribbean. "You're not—"

"You *are* Ms. Carmichael?"

"Mr. Thornton?" She said softly, and her heart seemed to shatter.

"I am delighted to make your acquaintance." He tottered forward into what she realized was supposed to be a bow.

This was the man who would be swimming in warm waters soon, weaving through algae and coral reefs, and avoiding jellyfish and sharks?

He should be incredible.

This man wasn't quite what she expected.

She hadn't expected a man quite so old.

Or quite so rotund.

Hopefully he would squeeze into her diving costume. She pressed her lips together and calculated the spare inches of material.

She quelled any doubts and dipped down into a curtsy. "I am pleased to meet you, Mr. Thornton."

"Lord Thornton, actually." He fixed his pale blue eyes on her and ran his fingers through his unctuous gray hair. "Only a man of some importance can acquire an invitation here. I suppose you favor directing your attention on the lowlife of...oceans. Quite adorable."

Her smile wobbled.

"You are so young." The man's tongue flickered about his lips.

Well, at least it wasn't just she who imagined an age difference.

Lord Thornton scrutinized her with a thoroughness that made the hairs on her arms, practically bare given the fashion for cap sleeves, prickle. She wrapped her shawl more tightly around her shoulders.

Perhaps she was overreacting.

Hopefully.

If his gaze was thorough, that only meant he cared about the details, one of the first requirements in being a scientist.

"I look forward to speaking with you," Lord Thornton said.

"Good," she squeaked.

"Perhaps we might dance?" His gaze drifted once again to her meager bosom, made more defined by the shocking lack of fabric covering the upper portion of it.

She shifted her legs over the floorboards, and they creaked beneath her.

"I would rather not."

"Ah." Lord Thornton nodded knowledgeably. "Such seriousness! You are not the first woman to say that to me."

"I mean—I doubt we would get much conversation when we were dancing," Louisa hastened to add. "All those patterns, switching partners. Not to speak of the fact that others might overhear us."

"Ah... You desire privacy. I approve most whole-heartedly in your wanton American ways." He leaned closer to her, comfortable in invading her personal space. "The thought of you compelled me to journey to Brighton."

"Not the thought of science?"

"That too." His eyes lingered at her chest.

Perhaps he was simply trying to find something there. She abhorred the flatness of her chest.

She cleared her throat, and he withdrew his gaze from her bosom.

The fact did not seem to be an immense improvement since his gaze was quite distinctly resting on her lips.

She had no desire to ponder what nonsense might be ratcheting through his mind, but she was quite certain that whatever was causing his tongue to glide over his too-full lips, was not appropriate.

Pondering kissing might be a favorable quality in a partner, but it lacked desirability in a man more than twice her age with whom she'd broken etiquette to correspond over vital scientific research.

They had the chance to be at the forefront of a discipline devoted to marine life that expanded the work of classical and Renaissance scientists. Unlike Aristotle, who had never sailed across the Atlantic, Thornton would be able to observe species of fish swimming in their natural habitats, and not gutted, hauled up by some fisherman along with cod and trout.

Thornton would be able to observe which fish swam in schools, and which fish ventured alone. The diving helmet would enable him a far clearer glimpse of the ocean than any other scientist had been offered. Why was he not excited?

She sighed. Was it possible *she* was being unfair?

His roaming gaze might have a simple explanation: masculinity. Didn't everyone remark on her lack of understanding of society? Perhaps the manner in which cold shivers rippled through her spine was a natural, yet unnecessary unease, on parting with her most prized possession.

"I hope the regent makes an appearance soon." Lord Thornton's eyes continued to linger on her. "I am eager for bed."

No.

She refused to explain away his behavior. This conversation needed to be curtailed.

Immediately.

One would think that a man with his scholarly background would possess some sense.

"Shall we discuss your journey to the West Indies now? I have placed the diving helmet on *The Sapphire Princess* as we discussed in my last letter to you. It would have been far too unwieldy to bring here, and I would not want the regent's footmen to misplace it. If you would like me to explain how it works—"

"Oh, I would," Lord Thornton said. "Most assuredly."

She smiled, grateful he finally showed some interest.

"Let's explore this palace. Perhaps there's a spare bedroom upstairs in which we might *converse*." Lord Thornton leaned closer to her, providing her with a close view of his stark cravat, as she attempted not to inhale his lavishly applied cologne.

If he were so fond of rose gardens, he could find one to explore. *Alone.*

"That will not be necessary." She rather had imagined they'd conduct their discussion in private, had rather hoped that the tight throng of people would shield her from her mother's watchful gaze, but now the thought of being alone with him caused her stomach to tighten disagreeably.

"I left some papers on things you might research with the diving helmet," Louisa spoke rapidly. "You were quite vague when you answered my advertisement on your particular research interests, but I can assure you the helmet will be equally useful if you want to document dolphins or lobsters or simple fish. Whatever you desire."

"I am glad you are willing to accommodate my desires." Lord Thornton's thick lips widened, as if she'd said something charming, and Louisa forced her attention back to him. His beady eyes had softened, and the strange dewy look made her spine prickle.

"That's not what I said," Louisa said sternly. Her throat seemed to dry, and she took a hasty swallow of the lemonade, before remembering that she did not like it. The sour drink did not ease her uncertainty, and a lump thickened in her throat.

"Do not argue," Thornton said. "The quality is unattractive in women."

The bastard.

Her fists clenched together, and every muscle in her

body seemed to snap. The *ton* might criticize her behind her back, but she'd never anticipated that the research scientist she'd longed to meet all year would criticize her openly. "I am not attempting to be attractive!"

"Obviously." Thornton nodded. "That dress is not pretty. Even I can tell."

He should be discussing diving, not dresses.

She firmed her jaw, and thrust her eyes into a dark glower, the sort she'd seen the Dowager Duchess of Alfriston cast on occasion, but Thornton's face didn't redden. "At least you would not require any expenses for your upkeep."

"My upkeep?"

Thornton nodded solemnly. "Should I propose."

"And you plan to propose?" Outrage coursed through her, crashing through her veins at a greater speed than any tide coming in.

"If you impress me." He sterned his expression, and his eyebrows pushed together as if to demonstrate cannons pushing through the holes of a ship's deck. "My standards are high, and I will not tolerate disobedience."

Distaste surged through, breaking through her last attempt at maintaining some façade of calm. The man was abominable.

"You are most mistaken, my lord," she said coldly. "I have no desire to marry you."

He didn't need to know she was already engaged. He didn't need to know *anything* about her.

"Every young lady desires marriage. I will sway you," Thornton said. "I swayed my late wife too."

His eyes roamed her figure once more in that abhorrent manner with which Louisa had already become far too familiar. The man's blatant interest in her figure rivaled only his equally blatant disinterest in diving. She'd been misled. She'd spent so long dreaming of this man, and of what he might accomplish, but even conversing with him proved painful.

"I am not some ornament for you to gaze at," she said, her voice low and steely.

"Good thing too," the man declared. "For you would make a horrible one." He glanced at her hair. "I'm sure there's a better way to wear that. I wouldn't want to pass on that trait to my unborn children."

"I wouldn't want to give you any children at all. We are discussing diving."

"You mean that charming hobby of yours?"

"And that serious pursuit of yours." Louisa kept her voice firm through some miracle of self-control. "So you claim." The last word *may* have been somewhat sarcastic. Managing to not sound distraught, not sound angry, not sound incredulous was an achievement more incredible than swimming underwater for long periods of time.

The man didn't even prize it.

"Do you even know how to dive?"

"Good God, no. Far too cold. Impossible."

"You told me that you could dive in the Caribbean," her voice wobbled, and nausea rose in her throat.

"That fanciful notion of yours?" He scoffed, tilting his bulbous head, scarcely covered by his smattering of gray hair. "I simply saw you were a woman of some creativity. The ability for a woman to occupy herself is a quality to be most treasured."

Her legs quivered as if she'd found herself trapped on a ship in the middle of a typhoon. Her heart seemed to scurry off ahead of her, beating a quick rhythm, as if it were flapping its chambers in an attempt to fly.

"You lied about everything you told me."

The man's eyes narrowed, a fact abetted by their natural beadiness. "Now look here, you needn't get all huffy with me. I know what you're really interested in. Don't play coy with me."

He chuckled and took a noisy slurp of his drink. "You didn't expect an actual scholar to be interested in your silly scheme?"

He'd dismissed her dream, her hours, weeks, years of work to a girlish scheme. All her effort to design a diving helmet was reduced to something for a man of his considerable dearth of caliber to mock.

Her stomach tumbled downward, and she stepped toward the wall as if the cold wallpaper might provide some protection.

"Advertising for a strong, smart man in a journal." His chuckle evolved into an open guffaw. "We all saw you were a woman. We all know you were just looking for a husband."

"That's absurd! Utterly absurd."

"Lord," he said. "You really didn't think I was serious about that?"

"We had a deal," she reminded him. "I bought a ticket for you. With all my pin money! And I put the diving helmet on the ship. It's leaving tomorrow!"

"No man in his right mind would put on some strange concoction that a *woman* had crafted and sink into the ocean. The idea is mad. Mad!"

He was wrong. The helmet worked perfectly. She'd gone over the design with such thoroughness and had tested it so many times. And now it was on board a ship, a ship that might be managed by current or former pirates, and no one ever would be able to use it.

She stepped forward, conscious that her eyes must be glaring. Fury wound her fists together again and restraining herself from slapping him seemed an impossible feat. "How could you do this? I could have gotten someone else."

"Truly?" The man managed to maintain a bored expression. "Did someone else contact you about desiring to participate in your insane experiment?"

She blinked, absolutely appalled that the man was, for once, correct.

No one had.

"Thought so," he declared smugly. "At least there's still time to sample Brighton's women. I've found that there's always many offerings where there are sailors." He gazed at her again. "It will be nice to be with a woman with an actual bosom."

She inhaled sharply and crossed her arms over her chest.

Chapter Eight

L ouisa blinked furiously. No need for anyone to see how shaken she was.

The crowd erupted in cheers, and for a horrible moment Louisa believed they might have heard the faux-scientist's words.

"All hail Prince George," a man bellowed, and tension eased in Louisa's shoulders.

A stocky, well-dressed man she recognized from her brief presentation at court sauntered forward, and the guests near him dropped into curtsies and bows. The sudden lowering of finely attired torsos allowed her to spot her mother, and she marched toward her, away from all memories of the faux-scientist demolishing all her dreams with the callous efficiency of a man firing muskets.

"There you are, darling!" Her mother's voice sailed toward her. "Who was that man you were speaking to?"

She turned, relieved to see her mother, even if she was clasping onto the arm of the well-dressed Mr. Daventry.

"No one of any importance," Louisa said.

Her mother nodded. "Good. It wouldn't do to make your fiancé jealous."

Louisa tried to smile. She rather thought jealousy was not an emotion that Cecil would feel toward her. *One of many emotions.*

"I think I would like to leave early now," she said.

"Indeed?" Her mother darted a look to her new husband. "I suppose we could go—"

"You needn't worry. I'm quite capable of finding my way back," Louisa said. "It takes so long to get the carriage out, and the townhouse *is* close to the Marine Pavilion. You should enjoy yourself."

Her mother beamed. "Thank you. You can be so proud of yourself, my dear. All settled after all. No need to worry about dancing with any more men now."

"Splendid." Louisa chirped.

She made her way through the throng of people. The staircase was now empty, everyone gathering inside for a glimpse at the Regent, and she quickly changed from her slippers to something better equipped to handle Brighton's cobbled roads.

The slam of crisp air against her was almost welcome. Anything to distract her from the fact that all her hopes for her research were lost. She'd spent so long constructing and testing the diving helmet.

And soon she would be shipped off to Northern England with a husband who promised to never love her and with in-laws who would adamantly await babies that would never, could never, arrive.

Because the terrible truth was . . . she was romantic. Even though the fact embarrassed her. She wished she possessed the cold practicality of Lady Cordelia or even of Percival's new wife Fiona. For though both were happily married neither of them had expected to be. Cordelia had resigned herself to an unhappy marriage, and Fiona had expected no marriage at all. It hadn't mattered to Fiona—she'd had her research.

And though Louisa adored nothing so much as diving and recording her findings, she'd always secretly longed for . . . more. That urge had only intensified after she'd witnessed the joy her brother had found.

It had seemed silly to her to force herself into an uncomfortable role. If she should marry, shouldn't it be someone with whom she could converse, whose company she might enjoy?

Perhaps she should not have discussed topics that the men would be unfamiliar with. Perhaps she should have restrained her comments to that of horses and the weather, venturing into a discussion of politics only after she'd assessed the likely opinion of her potential suitor beforehand, so as to best agree with him.

She'd always adored her family. Adored her sisters and brothers, despising only that she so rarely saw Percival and Arthur. She'd imagined one day having a house bustling with children.

Cecil excluded the possibilities of such daydreams turning to reality.

She wrapped her gloved arms together and held them against her chest.

If only she could delay the wedding! She was certain Percival or Arthur would not desire her to be miserable. Yet at the same time—even if her brothers supported their spinster sister, she did not want to burden them.

Her sister-in-law was pleasant, but Fiona possessed little inclination to attend balls and immerse herself in the *ton* as would be required of a proper chaperone.

Now Fiona had a new child in addition to her archaeological work.

She strode past the English Channel. The waves' familiar hum as they climbed the shore no longer soothed her, and she ached for the chance to explore once more under the sea's surface.

The Sapphire Princess sat regally in the sea. Moonlight shone over the masts and riggings, and she longed to once again set foot upon the hull and smell the scent of spruce and pine and run her fingers over the immaculately shaped vessel.

"Miss Thornton?" A deep, sultry voice called out.

*

What on earth is Miss Thornton doing there?

Rupert stepped toward the slender woman, swathed in a gown that glittered under the moonlight. She'd flung a shawl over her shoulders, and the silk edges fluttered under the brisk Brighton breeze.

Any other woman might be wary of standing so near the channel, where the wind was known to be strongest. No chaperone or maid seemed to be in sight.

Perhaps she'd just said farewell to her brother, and he glanced at the bay. Some shore boats pushed through the water in the direction of the anchored ships. The man must be on one of them.

The woman remained still, and he wondered if he'd made a mistake. A few link boys carried torches for their wealthy clients, and the bright, flickering lights illuminated her figure. It certainly appeared to be her, though the woman he'd met had not been clothed in such finery. The frizzy locks he remembered were tamed into a bun, topped with soft curls. Her expression remained solemn, and her profile still curved in that familiar manner: all sharp planes defined by high, soaring cheekbones.

"Miss Thornton?" He repeated.

Only now did the woman turn around, and the defiant certainty present in her gaze previously seemed to have subdued.

"Captain Rosse." She nodded to him. "I was deep in thought. All prepared for the voyage?"

"Aye," he said. "It will be nice to be under some decent sun again."

"The Caribbean sounds heavenly," she murmured.

"Maybe one day your brother can take you," he said.

"Well—" She looked like she wanted to say something more, but instead she shook her head. "That would be a pleasant dream."

She looked so wistful that he almost had an urge to comfort her. Instead he considered his life. He was an earl, though he was quite happy allowing most people to believe he had died in the Napoleonic Wars. "I've come to realize that it's good to go after one's dreams."

She smiled, and something about the slow upturning of her lips made his heart swell. "You are quite right, Captain."

"Looking for a ride?" A rower shouted from a shore boat, and Rupert answered in the affirmative.

He turned to Miss Thornton. "Your brother is in safe hands."

She seemed to hesitate again, but she only said, "I wish you a pleasant journey."

*

She should have told him she did not have a brother called Mr. Thornton. She should have told him that he wouldn't have a passenger.

But she didn't want to admit it to him. It seemed so pleasant to maintain the illusion that she might one day visit the Caribbean.

Goodness! She would adore such an opportunity. Not that the captain would ever allow it. Even stepping onto the ship this afternoon had been deemed eccentric. No captain in his right mind would allow an unmarried woman to travel by herself, without the permission of her parents, on a ship filled with men. The responsibility to defend her maidenhood would be far too great.

If only she could go herself and do the work. It wasn't just that men were allowed to peruse science and women were not. If only . . . She smiled. The captain had never met Mr. Thornton.

For one moment she imagined wearing masculine clothes and announcing to the captain that she was Mr. Thornton herself. Becky had even told the captain that Mr. Thornton was her brother. If she could somehow disguise herself . . .

She bit a lip to withhold a giggle.

Undoubtedly that thought could firmly be relegated to the absurd.

Even if she'd never possessed the female form depicted in paintings. Even if her chest and hips didn't splay in a manner men found enticing. Even if her voice was never likened to that of an angel, and she and her sister's governess had always instructed her to play the male role in any readings. Even if. . .

Sir Seymour had said she appeared masculine. And

though the fact had infuriated her, perhaps she could make use of the slim width of her hips. Perhaps for a few blissful weeks, it wouldn't matter if her complexion was unlikely to be compared to rose petals.

Perhaps the thought was not as absurd as she'd imagined.

Perhaps it was actually feasible.

She'd need to find the proper clothes, but there were male servants in the townhouse they'd rented . . .

All she needed were some breeches and a shirt.

Perhaps her mother would worry, perhaps she'd be furious, but Louisa would be content to suffer the consequences as long as she finally saw the Caribbean, finally did her research—this time herself, not needing to trust someone else.

And if Cecil still wanted to marry her . . . perhaps she could succumb to that plan. She'd have lived her dream.

For the first time that night hope surged through her.

Chapter Nine

Breeches dangled from a neighboring home's laundry line. The breeches were in themselves not vastly enticing. The quality was unremarkable: likely the pair belonged to one of the footmen. But now they seemed the most delightful things in the world.

The breeches swayed in the breeze, shoved between other masculine items. The plain linen managed to signify everything mysterious.

She'd never stolen before, and yesterday she wouldn't have thought it likely she would start with worn attire.

Louisa raised the sash window and clambered over the ledge. It was not the first time she'd left her home in this fashion. A forbidden passion for swimming in the ocean rather demanded a liberal relationship with house exits.

The wind brushed against her, and seagulls squawked to one another. They circled the cloud-strewn sky, the sole witnesses to her actions. The servants would be eating in the kitchen, and her mother would be sleeping after their late night.

Louisa hopped onto the ground. The hem of her gown

brushed against the smattering of flowers, still damp with dew and last night's rain.

She grabbed the unfamiliar male garments from the clothesline and sprinted back to her bedroom window. Her heartbeat sailed, as if billowed forward by potent gales, and she clambered inside. She hastened from the window and flung the attire on her bed.

If any of Louisa's etiquette books had thought it possible that a woman might stride about in breeches, that practice would likely have gone straight to the top of the list of things women must never do.

Instead none of the leather tomes her mother owned forbade the behavior. They hadn't contemplated that one of their readers might even ponder something so scandalous. They preferred to concentrate on the dreaded possibility of eating with the wrong fork or stretching one's arm to an unladylike extent for a sweet.

Louisa had broken rules before, continuing to research when she shouldn't, commissioning the construction of the diving helmet...but this exceeded everything in terribleness. Perhaps she'd long ago given up the attempt to be a respectable debutante.

It likely wasn't a good thing that breaking the rules, or even behaving in an unladylike manner came naturally to her.

The breeches seemed to stare threateningly at her from the bedspread, and she stretched her hand to it. Just touching the coarse cloth material seemed outrageous, how could she ever wear it?

But if she didn't...

None of the sailors knew the contents of the package. None of them might conduct research with it.

And none of them would care.

She stared at the mirror and lifted her hair back experimentally. She smiled.

Arthur was in Falmouth. She could join him there. Her mother would be horrified that she'd made the journey to Jamaica on her own, but she would at least not be arriving in the West Indies on her own. All she had to do was convince the crew of *The Sapphire Princess* of her masculinity. Given the fact that nobody had seemed impressed with her femininity, perhaps this was something she could do.

She'd already taken the clothes. She might as well wear them. She strode to her bed and shed her gown. She shivered more than the weather warranted and reached for the clothes.

She attempted to inhale deeply, but her breath seemed caught at the top of her throat, and her fingers trembled.

She firmed her lips and stepped into the breeches hastily. She pulled the shirt over her head, and her fingers fumbled as she tied the top. Her heartbeat quickened as if protesting the foreign fabric cut. She smoothed the strange shape of the attire and turned toward the mirror.

Probably she would look ridiculous.

Probably she would have to return the clothing.

Probably she'd succumbed to foolish dreams.

How could she feign being a man?

And yet...

When she peered into the mirror, her reflection was not as ridiculous as she'd feared. She turned slowly in the mirror, but her hips and chest were of such a natural narrow width that they did not give her away.

She turned around again.

No, this would work. Her face's sharp angles had never

seemed particularly feminine, and if no one wondered at the smoothness of her face, she might be successful.

She could always confess an abhorrence of sideburns. Her lips twitched.

She turned gingerly, as if any sudden movements might shatter the illusion.

But that would be impossible. Because it was her. In the mirror. Dressed like an average servant. A servant of the masculine variety.

She'd never felt more exposed. Yards of fabric were absent, and she'd never thought she'd miss the vibrant colored dresses her mother selected for her, as if her lack of suitors resulted from the fact they couldn't spot her.

Her limbs had never felt more visible. There was a gap between her legs. An actual gap, and her breeches hugged her legs in a scandalous manner.

Except it wouldn't be scandalous. Not when everyone thought her a man. It would be perfectly normal. Not worth a second glance.

She pulled her hair into a tight queue, though the thick strands bulged. Queues were old-fashioned, and she had a decided preference for the short hair the captain wore, but no one needed to think her fashionable. They just needed to think her a man. At least the austere hairstyle emphasized the angles in her face, and for the first time she was thankful for the plainness of her appearance. Her lips might be too thin, her jaw might be too wide, her cheekbones too low, but that didn't matter.

Her voice was a natural alto, but now she addressed her reflection in an even lower pitch. "Good morning."

She blinked, taken aback by her resemblance to a man. She swiveled before the mirror, and then her eyes scrutinized her chest.

Though her figure tended toward the narrow, a fact that her mother fought by putting her into over-sized gowns in a misguided hope that the extra material might create curves, her shirt *did* curve in a dangerous fashion. *Fiddle-faddle.*

She needed something, anything, to bind her bosom and broaden her waist. Clearly the servant had not included anything like that in his wardrobe. But perhaps—her gaze landed on her tablecloth. The plain white cotton, displaying a puritanical austerity, tempted her in a manner that would have appalled its maker.

She removed the objects from the table and lifted the cloth. She removed her shirt and pulled the thick fabric around her chest. The slope of her bosom and curve of her waist decreased.

Perfect.

She pulled her shirt over her torso again, looped the cravat into a simple knot and turned in front of the mirror.

Her family would be confused, perhaps even distraught at her disappearance.

But she couldn't *not* do this. She couldn't abandon her diving material on that ship when no scientist was there to make use of it. She couldn't just allow her mother to marry her off in a match always doomed to be loveless.

If they were so enthusiastic to rid themselves of her, her leaving for the West Indies would certainly suffice.

She stared at her tightly drawn back hair. The style could not be praised.

She sighed. They would just have to think her unstylish. Scientists were not renowned for their fashion sense, and she would just have to hope that sailors would be equally unfashionable.

The room lightened. Soon the sun would dash upward

in full force, light would spread over the horizon and Louisa might be discovered. She penned a quick note to her mother, telling her that she had gone to visit her brother. Likely they would think she'd gone to see Percival, not believing she would venture to Jamaica by herself.

She snatched her satchel and thrust her most treasured texts inside. If only she had more changes of clothes... She frowned. Perhaps there was one advantage to the fact that her stepfather visited her mother at night.

She opened the door to his room carefully. If he caught her... But the bed was empty, and she quickly grabbed some clothes and threw them into the bulging satchel. She snuck back into her room, raised the sash window and scrambled outside.

For the first time there was no need to lift her hem as she stepped over the flowers. She hastened across the street, accompanied only by the clonking of her too-large boots against the tile stones. If only she'd had the foresight to stuff stockings inside the toes.

Vibrant roses and peonies fluttered in the breeze, not hampered by their limited plots, perhaps even benefited by their proximity to their minders' doors. The Georgian townhomes that the elite of society rented when they felt the urge to leave London loomed beside her, and she focused her gaze ahead, wary that a bored aristocrat might draw back a drape and recognize her.

The members of the *ton* were clearly still in bed. Even those who hadn't secured an invitation at the Marine Pavilion would still be exhausted from private soirees. Some servants scurried past her, and she ducked her head down and attempted to blend with them.

Soon she would be there.

Soon everything would change.

Hopefully.

No way would she allow herself to be sent back home now. Not wearing breeches. That was enough to damage her reputation irreparably, more than any month-long absence. The air grew saltier, and she inhaled and rounded the corner.

The ocean lay before her. Shore boats thrust easily through the waves, and sailors swarmed over the deck of *The Sapphire Princess.*

Piles of dried seaweed squatted on the dock, likely thrown from a particularly bad storm. Fishermen swarmed over the wooden planks, and Louisa tensed.

They'd seen her visit the dock every day this week. If even one person recognized her—

She didn't want to contemplate such a catastrophe, and she focused her gaze on the ship that soared before her, bobbing in the ashen waves.

Her heart scuttled and scampered against her ribs, but she consciously slowed her pace.

Scientists weren't known for their habit of running through the streets

She strode purposefully toward the ship, and her heart thudded with a sound that rivaled her boots striking the planks. She peered at the tall mast that seemed to tower over the other ships, with their journeys limited to the continent.

She could do this.

She directed one of the people on the shore to row her to the ship. She half-expected the man to mock her, but he seemed oblivious to the strangeness of her attire.

She reached for her skirt as she grasped the ladder that led to the ship.

But she didn't have one, and she smiled, wondering at all the things men did not need to concern themselves with. She ascended the ladder and poked her head above the deck.

"Morning!" A sailor boomed a greeting toward her, and she forced herself to wave, as if it were the most normal thing in the world for her to be boarding a ship to the West Indies wearing breeches.

Somehow she'd assumed the sailors would be portly, bearded fellows like the fishermen in Salem. But these sailors weren't stranded in tiny boats for long hours of the day, with only food and drink to comfort them. These sailors had golden skin and moved with confidence over the deck.

Her heart thudded in her chest, and she clutched the side of the ship with an unnecessary vigor.

The only men she'd seen without their shirts had been stone statues.

She pulled her hat slightly more firmly over her head and avoided staring at the sailors' muscular torsos. At least she didn't spot the red-headed sailor and the overly arrogant, *definitely* overly handsome, captain.

She'd found that men had a habit of claiming the most space they could, perhaps to make up for the dearth of flowing fabric draped around women, and she strove to mimic the confidence of their walk.

Fortunately her dance instructors had always remarked on her lack of elegance, and it took little effort for her to mimic a clumsy stride, one unconcerned with which direction her toes pointed.

The sailors emitted profanities as carelessly as most people used regular words. The language grated on her ears, but she refused to falter. Men were accustomed to this.

She glanced toward the dock, but no other passengers followed her onto the ship. She was alone.

With about twenty large, brawny men.

The towering masts sent a thrill throttling through her, and her heart thudded happily as she ambled beneath the elaborately arranged rigging.

She wondered at each carefully constructed detail, enhanced after centuries of experience on the seven seas.

"Don't just stand there," a gruff sounding voice barked, and she jumped despite her best attempts. Perhaps men were always shouting at other men. Perhaps that was something that wouldn't irritate them in the least.

"What are you doing?" The sailor continued. "Come to deliver anything?"

"No."

He swept his gaze over her and scowled. He was tall, and his skin was so dark she suspected he might possess some Caribbean blood. Perhaps a pirate father had bedded one of the dark-skinned women depicted on illustrations in her books on the West Indies. "We're a busy ship, lad. We're about to set sail."

"I know." Louisa swallowed hard and glanced at the shore boat, still nearby.

They were still anchored.

She could fetch the diving helmet and return home.

But this was her chance. Her only chance in all the world to visit the West Indies and conduct research herself. She hadn't been able to trust Mr. Thornton and perhaps she would never find anyone with the capabilities to carry out her research to believe her.

This is the moment.

"I'm a passenger," she said.

His brows scrunched together. "You're Mr. Thornton?"

"Indeed," Louisa said in her most authoritative voice, striving to maintain a deep pitch. "I am expected here."

The sailor peered at her again, and his lips curled into a frown. The faint scent of rum and tobacco and all things forbidden wafted toward her.

Only a few feet separated them, and she widened her stance to mimic the territorial instinct of the other sex. She met his eyes, careful not to hide behind fluttering eyelashes.

"Reckon you look awfully young to be a doctor," the sailor said.

"It's my skin. It's quite decent." She hesitated. "The knowledge that I obtained as a scientist helped me maintain it."

"Hmph," the sailor said. "Don't know scientists that desire to look young. Would have thought you lot went more for the respectable look. Beards and such."

Louisa frowned and channeled the easily enticed outrage of a man. "I hope you do not mean that you find me lacking respectability?"

"No, er—" The sailor shook his head. "I'll, er, show you to the captain."

Louisa tensed.

She'd met the captain. They'd spoken together, even if she had been attired very differently. If he recognized her...

She'd hoped that she might avoid seeing him until it was too late for him to dismiss her from the ship.

She waved her hand loftily. "I do not have time for your administrative matters. Please direct me to my cabin."

The sailor frowned.

"I take it you know where my room is?" Louisa asked.

"Course I know jes where it is," he said.

The outraged tone made her lips swerve upward involuntarily. Men seemed to be in a constant state of defending their pride, and this sailor was no exception.

"I'll, er, show you downstairs."

He believes me.

She turned away lest he startle at the happiness that must be visible in her facial muscles.

She'd spoken with him, and though he'd growled and grumbled, he hadn't found fault in the pitch of her voice or the curve of her body, and he certainly hadn't accused her of any misdeeds.

"We're 'appy to 'ave you 'ere," the sailor said gruffly, avoiding her eyes.

"Excuse me?"

"I said we're happy to have you," the sailor repeated at a higher volume, still avoiding her eyes. "The captain told me to tell the passengers that."

"How kind of him," Louisa said after a pause.

"Personally I think it would be better to have no passengers," the sailor grumbled and gestured for her to follow him. "Passengers are more troublesome than crates of furniture or barrels of rum."

She scurried after the man, descending the steeply sloped stairs.

She stretched her hands to her thighs as she descended the steps before remembering she had no hem to lift. The sailor did not remark on her inelegant gait. Men were likely not admonished for any overhasty wardrobe decisions or spurts of clumsiness. Even the clanking of her boots was obscured by the heavier thuds from the sailors working above deck and thundering through the passageways.

When they descended the stairs, they ducked their heads underneath the low ceiling. The sailor marched forward unperturbed by the constrained space. She supposed he was accustomed to do even more athletic activities to fulfill his duties than duck his head on occasion.

"You're our only passenger," the sailor announced, stopping before a door.

"Splendid," she replied, keeping her pitch low.

Probably the dearth of other passengers to interact with was a good thing. No passengers meant more time to peruse her beloved tomes and less time worrying about whether her appearance lacked sufficient masculinity.

Louisa shifted her feet against the floorboards, and the sailor knocked on the door. Louisa stiffened. If this was her room, why exactly was he knocking? A queasy feeling, not one explained by the slight dip as waves lapped against the hull, pervaded her.

*

Rupert swung open his door.

Conrad stood before him with some skinny man in a poorly tied cravat.

"This is our passenger." Conrad jerked his thumb at the stranger and flashed Rupert a wide grin, the kind usually given reluctantly during consultations with the ship's surgeon.

The scientist had arrived.

Brilliant.

He'd hoped for more passengers and had worried when

he'd returned to the ship last night and did not find Mr. Thornton. But one passenger was a start, and maybe the man would lead to more people.

Anything to keep him from succumbing to hauling the more questionable and downright dreadful cargo from the West Indies that some captains were forced to do.

Rupert was determined to show this man a good time.

"Mr. Thornton," he said. "I'm Captain Rosse."

"But we 'ere jes call him Cap'n," Conrad said, somewhat unhelpfully.

The scientist, who greatly resembled his sister, avoided his eyes. Likely he was taken aback by Conrad's blatant familiarity. He knew the upper class. He knew what pride they took in stringent hierarchies, defending them with a vigor better suited for defending the ever-expanding borders of the British Empire.

"We do tend toward informality here," Rupert explained.

The only thing he regretted was not breaking those outdated systems earlier. Any of these men were worth more than the brandy swishing gentlemen with whom he'd grown up, who spent their time moaning about their servants

"I've met your sister," Rupert said.

"G-good." The stranger gave him a wobbly smile though his eyes had the same expression that foxes had—or should have—right before they were going to be shot.

Rupert grinned. This was going to go a whole lot better than he thought. The man seemed too meek to be too demanding. He'd suspected yesterday that the woman on board had exaggerated her brother's strengths.

"Follow me," Rupert said magnanimously. "I'll show

you the ship. Ever been on one before? But you're American, and in England, so you must have."

The scientist's eyes widened as if he hadn't expected to be the focus of any conversation.

His eyes and the curve of his nose resembled his sister greatly.

Not that he could see much. Mr. Thornton seemed intent on fiddling with his cap.

"That's your cabin." Rupert gestured to the door beside his quarters.

"Wonderful," the scientist squeaked, and then coughed. "I trust my—er—package is there? My—er—sister dropped it over."

Rupert nodded, and his shoulders relaxed though he still seemed jittery.

"It's perhaps best if I ascertain for myself."

Rupert's lips twitched, and he gestured for Fergus to open the room. He hesitated at the door, unsure what Mr. Thornton might make of the sparsely decorated room, but the scientist only strode to the brown package and unwrapped it.

Rupert hovered in the corridor, not used to being so thoroughly ignored, but Mr. Thornton soon turned around and beamed. "It's here."

"Naturally," Rupert said, smiling back at him.

The scientist's smile wobbled, and his eyes lowered.

People Rupert encountered generally did not suffer any timidity. That was not a trait that led people to board ships destined to far corners of the globe. Mr. Thornton seemed to be even intimidated, and for one horrible second, it occurred to Rupert that the man might know his position.

But that was unlikely. He'd been so careful.

Scientists were supposed to be the very best types of passengers. So devoted to their work that they didn't have a moment to consider anything else, and so accustomed to being teased for their tendency to find the most obscure things appealing, that they refrained from disparaging others.

"You are welcome to stay and...read. But you also are welcome to join me on the deck."

He knew which answer Thornton would choose. Rupert had been on ships for so long that he knew when a person found ships compelling or when they saw them as a form of transport to be tolerated with only a great tirade of complaints.

This man belonged to the former category. He'd seen the pleasure that had crossed over his face when entering the cabin, and how his eyes had lingered on *The Sapphire Princess*'s design.

"And see the ship leave the port?" The scientist's excitement compelled Rupert to smile.

"It's always my favorite portion of the journey," Rupert confessed. Most captains professed a preference for calm waters, and in truth, he enjoyed the times when the sails were already out, when the wind was strong, when the sailors were in their berths, that he might stride about on the deck and imagine the ship belonged entirely to him. But there was something thrilling about when the sailors were hoisting everything into position. They were in a machine. Every portion of the ship had been thought about, refined from years, decades, centuries of experience on the sea.

"I'll explain everything to you," Rupert said benevolently, and Conrad tilted his head in obvious bemusement.

"Splendid," Mr. Thornton repeated.

"Some people will come to the dock to wave," Conrad said. "Jealous buggers."

Mr. Thornton seemed to flinch, but then he shrugged. "On second thought I'll just remain here."

"You don't want to see the ship depart?" Rupert asked.

"No." Mr. Thornton flashed them another wobbly smile.

"Perhaps he's seasick," Conrad mused. "That's why we didn't want no passengers. Passengers always get sick. And we ain't cleaners, we're sailors. If we wanted to clean, we would have been born women. Which we ain't." Conrad pointed in a downward direction, and his lips spread into a wide grin.

Mr. Thornton's face paled, and he lowered his satchel. It seemed to be bulging, and likely was too heavy for the man.

"Let him get settled." Rupert clapped Conrad on the shoulder.

Mr. Thornton nodded, and his hand stretched to his ear, as if he desired to tuck a strand behind it, and the man's face pinkened.

Perhaps Conrad was right, and the scientist would be confined to his cabin for the remainder of the journey with seasickness.

Chapter Ten

The ship rolled and began gliding from the town. Louisa stared at the closed door. No furious footsteps sounded, and her mother's strident voice did not holler her name.

She'd done it.

She'd actually done it.

She was on the ship, sailing to the Caribbean, and none of the crew had thought the fact unbelievable.

No one had noticed she was a woman. Not even the captain, though he had seemed to look at her strangely. No one had questioned her right to be here. No one had even mocked her for her research.

She settled onto the bed. She needed to be careful around him. The urge to melt under his gaze was overwhelming.

It would be nice to be on the deck, but she would stay in her cabin until they were farther from Brighton, on the off chance a fisherman might recognize her.

And she needed to do something about the space between her legs. The sailor's lewd gesture toward his own hefty masculinity had made that clear. She grabbed her satchel, grateful she'd packed her sewing kit. She would need to sew a false appendage onto her breeches.

She unpacked and removed some scientific journals, but for the first time, she couldn't concentrate on the articles.

When she returned she would be disgraced. So disgraced that perhaps even a baronet's son in Yorkshire in need of a wife might think twice of tying his life with hers, no matter how powerful her brother might be in England.

She smiled. That would be just fine.

In a few weeks she would see her brother Arthur again, and he would know what to do.

She would contemplate her future later. Now she would enjoy the present.

A knock sounded on the door, and Louisa leaped up

Would it be the captain? She brushed her hand against the tightly drawn queue. The novel texture made her frown.

"Mister?" A voice carried through the thin door easily, and Louisa sighed.

She remembered to deepen her voice. "One moment."

She unhooked the latch and swung open the door. A sailor stood before her carrying a tray of cold meats and bread. The man's ginger hair was unmistakable.

Fiddle-faddle.

She'd met him before. He'd been the sailor on the ship whom she and Becky had met.

"I'm Fergus. Welcome." The man's gaze narrowed, and he seemed to scan the planes of her face.

"I'm Mr. Sebastian Thornton," she said, maintaining a deep voice. Her heart pounded with the uneven ferocity of a rowboat caught in a storm, and she strove to compose her face into the bland expression demanded from debutantes at balls. He carried a tray with an array of bread, cheese, and cold meats. "You've brought food."

"Aye." The man nodded, as if she'd noticed something clever. "Cap'n Rosse thought you might be hungry."

"Oh." She smiled and took the tray, angling her head away from the man. "How very kind of the captain."

"Ah, he's a good captain," the man declared. "I've been with him from the very beginning."

"How nice." She wondered if that meant that the two men confided in each other.

"Pardon me, sir," Fergus said, and his voice toppled downward. "But you look mighty familiar."

Tension shot through her body, but she forced herself to give a lackadaisical shrug, even though the effort seemed to risk snapping her spine. "I'm sure I would remember you."

The man barked a laugh. "That's what everyone says. Was useful in my, er, past career. Scary and such."

She tilted her head, unsure why being noticeable had been an advantage. Most people desired to blend into the surroundings, not frighten them.

Becky's words ran through her mind. Had this really been a pirate ship?

The man's gaze remained fixed on her, and she shivered. She was pretty sure it was a bad idea to lie to pirates. It wasn't good to lie to anyone, but pirates at least likely veered toward violent inclinations when insulted. "My sister brought my diving helmet," she rushed to say. "Perhaps you met her?"

"You're right, mister." Fergus chuckled. "So I did. You be looking awfully similar."

Louisa nodded. "Quite easily explained."

She took the tray of food and placed it on the only table in the room, moving the articles and books she'd already placed there to the side.

"This looks good," she said.

The man smiled and revealed a line of gaily yellowed teeth, varying in shade and shape.

"'Tis the man's job to look after you. Yer the first passenger we've had," he declared. "I should tell 'im you think 'e's doing a good job!"

Louisa's eyebrows darted up. *How odd.* She wondered why Lady Rockport had recommended Mr. Thornton sail on this ship. The marchioness had been so happy to recommend it.

"'E says yer to dine with 'im tonight," Fergus continued.

"Oh?" Louisa's throat dried. Dinner with the captain was not unusual. Pity the man's apparent inexperience with passengers had not prevented him from that knowledge of propriety.

When Mama and she had sailed to England, they'd always dined with the captain. Then they'd always been in the presence of many other passengers. No other passengers, much less women, were on this ship.

She couldn't simply dine with him. The thought was absurd. She was still a woman. Spending time with him might lead to discovery. And women were certainly not supposed to dine alone with men.

And yet there was no reason in the world to decline his invitation.

Could she feign seasickness? *Not for a five-week journey.* And she certainly didn't want to make anyone suspicious.

"I'll be there," she said weakly.

"Jolly good." The sailor beamed and then hesitated. He dipped his torso into an awkward bow and then walked backward from the room.

They aren't used to passengers here.

She settled at the table and bit into the bread. The cabin had no window, and the cramped space and swaying floor were the only indicators she was at sea.

Time passed quickly nevertheless, and soon it was time to see the captain. She was wondering whether there was indeed an excuse she might make, when a knock sounded again.

"Mr. Thornton!" The captain's strong voice carried through the thin door easily, and tension shot through Louisa.

She unlocked the door, conscious of the slight tremor of her fingers.

He peered down at her, his lips set into a wide smile.

If only he were not quite so handsome.

He was taller than most other men, and his hair may once have been termed brown, though he'd clearly spent most of his time under a hot sun. Some of the strands were caramel colored, and she forced her gaze away from contemplating the shades of gold. His eyes were a deep blue color, as if she were looking into the ocean on the very loveliest day. She turned her head away, conscious that her heart rate was escalating to a degree not befitting that of a male passenger conversing with his all too masculine captain.

Adonises were best suited to reclining in clouds painted by Italian artists. They weren't supposed to be staring at her from below a captain's hat.

She cleared her throat and widened her stance into a

masculine pose. The gesture seemed ridiculous, but she'd witnessed other men adopt a similar position.

She wasn't going to give herself away now. Not when she was so near having her dream fulfilled.

The captain didn't blink though Louisa couldn't allow herself to relax in his presence. Relaxing might mean she spoke in her natural tone. Relaxing might mean she lingered her gaze on his for longer than appropriate. She smiled, though the gesture felt more tight and awkward than she would have desired.

The captain glanced at the table and stack of articles. "You must share your research with me."

"Oh!" She blinked. "I would be happy to do so."

She wasn't accustomed to people expressing interest in her work.

"Let's dine." He nodded matter-of-factly, and she followed him. There was no excuse for her to make, and despite the danger of being in his company, she was drawn to him.

The captain swung open the door to his room and stepped inside. She followed him, enjoying the novelty of holding the door open herself.

The captain's quarters were clearly the nicest part of the ship. Light shone from a row of windows, and blue-green waves crested below a now blue sky.

"How marvelous," she said.

The captain smiled. "Please sit."

The walls still seemed narrow and the ceiling low. Or perhaps it was simply the captain's presence that exuded throughout the room.

She settled at a long table, pulling the chair for herself.

She'd never been alone in the same room with a man before.

They were both men.

She was his only passenger.

It was completely, utterly natural to be alone with him.

And yet it didn't feel natural at all, and she was certain her mother and all the high society would find only things to criticize of the lack of other people around them.

Except she wasn't a debutante anymore.

She rested her hands over the table and glanced at the food. Bright carrots and Brussels sprouts were piled on platters. The smell of steak emanated through the air.

"I told cook to make some meat," he said cheerfully. "The advantages of fresh provisions."

Her lips twitched. Their meeting was likely of less interest to the captain than the food spread before them.

Though some men's coats did seem to ripple with the display of muscles, far too many seemed to ripple only from past feasts of lamb, and their elaborate cravats seemed merely to mask their multitude of chins.

Captain Rosse did not suffer from that affliction.

She forced her gaze away from him, searching for anything, absolutely anything, to distract herself from the deep blue shade of his eyes and the friendly crinkle of his skin when he smiled.

He poured some drink into her glass, and she hesitated, regarding the burgundy-colored liquid. Finally she raised it to her lips slowly.

"Stop."

She halted the ascent toward her lips. What had she done wrong? But he simply clinked glasses with hers. She tried not to notice the manner in which his muscles curved even underneath his attire, and she certainly tried not to mull over the curve of his cocky grin.

"So tell me about your research, Mr. Thornton." He sliced into his steak. She smiled and followed suit.

"I might bore you," she warned.

"I can always ask Fergus to make coffee if matters get too difficult."

She laughed, and her shoulders relaxed. This part was easy. She'd imagined this part all her life.

"I study marine life," she said, and her heart thumped more forcefully when he merely nodded. He did not joke that the subject might be seen as unbecoming to a woman, and his eyes did not widen to an extraordinary degree. The statement was only one to be respected, and not to be wondered at. "In fact I've created a diving helmet that will allow people to see underwater."

"Indeed?"

"Yes." She smiled.

"And you feel there is a need to see underwater?"

"If one desires to observe the life there," she replied. "There are a great many species of fish."

"And you find it important to observe them?"

"All life is fascinating, Captain Rosse. When I use the diving helmet, I am exploring a new world."

"You are fearless."

"I take pride in the construction of my diving helmet. I have tested it repeatedly."

He smiled. "I was referring to the many beasts in the ocean. The poisonous fish, the sharks, and the strength of the waves themselves."

"Oh." She blinked, and then her lips soared upward, and she had to hasten to take another sip of her drink lest she spend the rest of the night marveling at him.

He was the first person in her acquaintance to raise the possible dangers of her work. Her mother had warned her repeatedly of the dangers to her reputation, and her siblings and friends had expressed polite interest in her work, but it had not seemed to occur to anyone that she might be in danger.

"I am careful," she said.

"Most people who travel to the West Indies do not describe themselves in that manner."

"Perhaps I do have an adventurous streak," she admitted.

Captain Rosse didn't know the extent of it.

"But I find there is great value," she continued, "in learning about others."

"Even when the others cannot speak to you?"

She smiled. "Even so. In fact I intend to illustrate any new species I find."

"You paint?" The captain set his fork and knife down and stared at her. "How fascinating."

"I am not the only scientist doing this."

"And yet I imagine there are not many scientists depicting marine life."

"Perhaps not," she replied. If there had been, Mr. Thornton would not have been the only person to contact her.

"I am hopeful," she mused, "that the warmer water in the West Indies indicates a wider variety of marine life. I have heard reports of the increased variety of birds there and am eager to examine under the ocean's surface."

He tilted his head, and his dark locks rearranged themselves into a new, equally enticing pattern. "You must tell me what you find. You can show me your drawings."

She beamed and then quickly directed her gaze to her plate and the task of slicing her steak. It would not do to spend the entire evening gazing at him in rapture. Nobody had shown her studies such interest before.

She nodded. "Have you traveled to the West Indies often?"

"Some would say too often."

"It must be difficult for your parents," she mused, and the captain's easy-going expression tightened.

She cursed her forwardness, but the captain's face soon relaxed as he began speaking of the wonders of the islands, and she vowed not to press him.

Not everyone had parents.

Her father was dead—she should have known better than to assume his were alive and concerned about him.

"You will enjoy our journey to the Caribbean," the captain said. "You will find much of interest there. We will land in Barbados first, the oldest occupied British island."

"Ah."

"And then we'll visit St. Lucia." The captain grinned. "Personally that is my favorite."

"Because Britain has just recently won it?"

"I'm a proud Englishman," he declared. "And happy that we freed it from those wretched French."

"And then Falmouth?"

He nodded. "We'll circle back to the other islands though."

She wished she could join him on the entire journey, but Arthur was in Falmouth.

"I am looking forward to the voyage with all my heart." Her cheeks warmed, and it occurred to her that men might not be speaking about their hearts with as great a frequency as women did.

He only grinned, and she concentrated again on her plate.

They spoke more of the various islands, and he regaled her with tales of past battles. She gathered that he'd fought for the Royal Navy.

"So you're not a pirate?" she asked finally.

"Ah, you've been hearing the rumors then. I suppose that's befitting of a scholar. You must possess a great love for research." His eyes sparkled.

"Are you going to tell me if the rumors are true?"

"Do I look like a pirate?" He grinned further.

"Well. No." He looked quite respectable, not that musing aloud on the captain's appearance would be remotely appropriate.

"Good." The captain leaned toward him. "We were technically privateers. We passed a portion of our winnings to the crown. The main thing was, we helped keep foreign ships from lingering too near our islands."

"I'm not convinced that was respectable."

"Then you have good instincts." The captain grinned and tore off his cravat. Dark hair curled from the opening of his shirt, and Louisa fought the obscure urge to trace his neck with her fingers.

Chapter Eleven

They'd finished supper, and generally when dining with others Rupert would eventually clear his throat and mention something about work.

This time was different. Rupert found he had no urge to usher the scientist out. Something about the man amused him, and he poured some rum.

He clinked his crystal tumbler against the scientist's. "Cheers."

"Cheers." The scientist took a generous swallow, and then his eyes widened, and he plunked the crystal tumbler down with such force that the amber liquid sloshed over the rim. "It burns."

"Aye." Rupert had to bite away the urge to laugh. What person had not drunk spirits?

There was something familiar in the scientist's large gray eyes, and his eyelashes seemed uncommonly long. His cheeks darkened, and he seemed more intent on pondering the assorted artwork fastened onto the wall than directing his gaze at Rupert's.

Rupert relaxed into his chair. Perhaps his passenger

had made a name for himself studying marine life, but he seemed uncommonly ill at ease with the practices of actual life.

Mr. Thornton reminded him of the more dedicated students at Harrow, the ones who seemed to genuinely delight in reciting Latin poems, and who seemed spurred on for an actual desire for knowledge rather than avoiding the tutors often brutal wrath.

The fact made him smile, and he sipped more rum. He hadn't ruminated on his time at school in years.

He'd prepared himself for the pontifications of a scientist, and he'd steeled himself for the easy disparagements of a man who deemed those surrounding him lacking. In his experience, so-called intellectuals suffered from a dearth of knowledge on all life matters not tampered by an insistence of their superiority.

And yet when he spoke with him, he did not mourn the absence of a merchant or other seaman.

People became scholars because they were able to reason better than other men and because they found their stacks of books provided comfort. They did not require the glory that so many of Rupert's navy comrades had sought, the glory that Rupert had sought himself.

His father had been reluctant to let him go. He'd been too aware that Rupert hadn't sired an heir, and even the threats of Bonaparte barging onto Britain's borders hadn't dispelled his father's notion that Rupert would be better off at home, a member of the local militia, but certainly never a member of the army.

When Rupert had joined the navy, his father wished he'd joined the army.

His father would have liked to have purchased him an

officer's position, using his influence to station him with other well-born men who might become useful to him.

The navy was everything his father had despised.

The navy was a meritocracy, and the sailors had scoffed when Rupert had appeared in his early twenties. Most sailors his age already had ten years of experience, and Rupert had struggled those first months.

He smiled.

He'd learned. And of course, he'd had Jasper by his side. His chest clenched, as it always did when he considered his former best friend.

In truth, most of the men traveling to the West Indies were rabid opportunists, happy to spend the evening itemizing their land acreage, when they had some, or detailing extensively their dreams of acquiring the vast wealth that the Creoles had attained. Their eyes glistened when they spoke of sugar, and he knew it was not the sweetness they were contemplating. They spoke disparagingly of some people's desires to purchase sugars from French and Dutch colonies and of the idealists who hoped to curb the slave trade which the plantations depended on.

The man returned his gaze to the paintings of the Caribbean.

"That one is of Falmouth, isn't it?" The scientist pointed to one.

"You are knowledgeable in things besides fish."

The scientist's cheeks pinkened. The gesture caused him to wonder. He didn't expect such modesty, and somehow the gesture seemed charming.

"You are far more well-traveled," Mr. Thornton said. "I am envious. There is so much I would like to see."

"More even than visiting the West Indies?"

"Much more." He sighed. "Though I will content myself with that. Those destinations are more than I could ever have hoped for in life."

Rupert chuckled. "Most people count the days until they can leave the ship."

"Then most people are foolish."

"That is likely the case."

Rupert winked and unwound his cravat, and Mr. Thornton blushed again.

Perhaps he had some skin affliction.

The man's eyes seemed fixed on him, and then he swallowed hard. "I—I should retire."

"This is the first night on your journey. Surely you can enjoy yourself."

"Well..." The scientist bit his lower lip, and Rupert pulled his gaze away from the sudden crushing of white teeth against pink. The vulnerable gesture stirred something in him. Something he associated more with being in the presence of women. He frowned. Perhaps he was confusing Mr. Thornton with his sister. That would make sense, since he'd met her first.

His shoulders relaxed, and he allowed himself to smile. "Tell me about your sister."

"My sister?" The man sounded startled.

"I met her, remember?"

"Ah, yes." The man gave an uneasy smile.

Thornton certainly lacked the easy brashness of most passengers.

But then again, this man was a scientist and was likely unaccustomed to people. He likely favored test tubes and neatly written records. Just because the man was enthusiastic at being at sea did not mean the man had rid himself of all his shyness. He'd told his crew to treat

Mr. Thornton with honor, but the poor men were more accustomed to plundering and inspiring fear in others, and it was inevitable that they might seem intimidating.

He frowned, hoping he did not seem intimidating either. Perhaps there was more to being a good host than shaving one's beard.

"This is your home now," Rupert said, seeking to reassure the fellow. "Just imagine that this is your parlor, and I am your brother."

A strange expression flitted over the scientist's face, but he nodded. "Yes."

Rupert smiled. The ship swayed as it cut through the waves, and he took another sip of rum. He shifted on his seat.

Bloody French chairs. He wished he'd had the foresight to seize a Dutch ship. Dutchmen tended to be large.

He leaned back, stretching his arms over his head and arching his chest.

Mr. Thornton gasped and withdrew his gaze away from Rupert with such haste that Rupert wondered if he'd spilled food over his shirt. But when he looked in the mirror, everything seemed ordinary.

Perhaps Thornton did not care for Englishmen. He wouldn't be the first American to feel that way, and that would certainly explain his obvious discomfort. Rupert had fought against Americans in the War of 1812 when America had continued to send ships to France, as if completely incognizant of the destruction that Bonaparte was making over all of Europe, all the world. Perhaps all the talk about battling in the Royal Navy had made the man uncomfortable.

Rupert had been proud to serve Britain, but he knew some Americans felt less forgiving, even now, of the war.

Mr. Thornton would have grown up despising the English. Naturally he would feel a modicum of discomfort.

He sighed.

Naturally that would be the cause. He had to admit to some feelings of prejudice himself. It was foolish for them to act otherwise. Who knew how many of Mr. Thornton's relatives the Royal Navy had slain. Mr. Thornton might be from New England, might be from a region of the former colonies that never desired war, but that could not mean he was insensitive to its effects.

He despised that he'd felt a similar unease with Americans. Naturally the man must be uneasy to be with a British man. The war had scarcely ended.

"Let's get this into the open," Rupert said. "I know your secret."

The scientist's cheeks darkened, and for a moment his lower lip wobbled.

Some strange wave of tenderness ratcheted through Rupert.

Mr. Thornton tilted his head, further exposing his tightly drawn queue. Golden candlelight flickered over his soft features.

Rupert pulled his gaze away. "I know your behavior. It's—well, I don't want you to do it. I don't think there should be any secrets between us. We're going to be spending lots of time together."

The scientist squirmed in his seat, and his eyes seemed to widen even further.

"You mustn't worry," Rupert continued. "In fact, I share your secret too."

"What?" Thornton blinked, his horror evident. More sympathy rushed through Rupert.

"These days it's quite common," Rupert said, contemplating his experience fighting Americans.

For a long moment the scientist just stared at him. Finally, he broke his gaze. "You don't show it."

"I would hope not! I wouldn't be able to do my job if I did." He intended to continue taking passengers overseas, even if they were of the former colonial variety.

"I can imagine that," the scientist nodded. And then he gave a warm laugh. "I don't believe you at all."

"You should," Rupert said more quietly, and his tone sobered. "I want to apologize if I seemed intimidating before. It's just—I'm not used to being in so close quarters to a person—"

"Like me?" The scientist's wry smile pained Rupert's heart, and he wrapped his arms to cover his chest.

Rupert nodded. "It's not your fault."

"Some people would say it was," Mr. Thornton said miserably.

"That's dreadful! You can't help what you're born!"

"Goodness me!" Mr. Thornton buried his face in his hands.

Rupert absentmindedly noted the slenderness and almost daintiness of the man's hands. Perhaps they were more smooth because he worked with his mind.

Something stirred in his body, but Rupert ignored it. After all, it was natural for him to admire a person's hands who didn't work. Pure curiosity.

It had simply been a long time since Rupert had socialized with non-sailors.

Mr. Thornton wouldn't be the only man he met who shared this trait. Merchants weren't known for bouts with physical labor either. Now that he no longer made his fortune as a privateer he would become acquainted with more men with this feature. Rupert was simply musing on that fact. Life changes tended to make one reflective.

He poured himself another drink, though the familiar splatter of amber liquid against crystal did not ease the quickened thumping of his heart.

His mind had sought strange places this evening.

Maybe he really should return to England for good.

He'd been on a ship for too bloody long.

He enjoyed his work, but maybe it made sense to have something...more.

The scientist's face seemed to have gone an unnaturally light pallor.

Blast.

"Forgive me. I shouldn't have told you that I noticed," Rupert said.

"Oh. I—I suppose it's good you told me." The scientist bowed his head, and his fingers pattered a nervous rhythm over the wooden table. "Do you think anyone else knows?"

Rupert pondered it. He'd like to say no, but that wouldn't be quite honest. Everyone remembered the war, and the scientist had locked himself in his room all day. He stroked his chin.

"Probably," he admitted.

"Fiddle-faddle!" The scientist's narrow shoulders sank further. He seemed so weak compared to the other sailors, though Rupert already knew that Mr. Thornton outshone them in knowledge. "No one said anything."

"I have a polite crew," Rupert said with some pride. Perhaps other ships might have less reasonable crew members who could not understand the merits of tolerance.

"An *extraordinarily* polite one," he said, and his eyes

widened in something that resembled awe. The open admiration warmed Rupert.

"Well!" Rupert grinned. "Perhaps."

The scientist's eyes sparkled, and Rupert turned his gaze away. It was perhaps unusual to contemplate their resemblance to the stars.

Probably his conscience was reminding him that he should go on deck before too long, where he might see some actual stars.

Yes, exactly.

"How did you train them so well?" Mr. Thornton asked, his voice still incredulous.

"To give them credit, I never actually discussed it with them," Rupert admitted. "But they know to give even the people different from them no trouble."

"That's wonderful."

His tone seemed to have attained a higher pitch, underscoring his surprise, and Rupert directed his eyes elsewhere.

"It's nothing," he said, but somehow, under the full force of the scientist's starry-eyed gaze, his heart squeezed as if it were important. "They know you can't help being American. I know it must be strange for you being on a ship with no Americans, just with your former enemies, but, the war is over now."

Mr. Thornton's fork clattered on his plate, and his cheeks darkened.

"I'm sorry," Rupert said hastily. "Perhaps you wanted to keep that a secret—but with your accent, I am surprised you would have thought they wouldn't have figured it out."

The man only smiled, and his shoulders eased as if relieved.

Chapter Twelve

She was American. And she might be uncomfortable being around her former enemies.

That's what he's discovered.

Not that she was a woman.

Louisa waited for the tinge of pleasure at remaining undiscovered.

In truth her shoulders did relax, and when she smiled, her lips did not wobble, and her heart did not careen wildly.

But for a few moments, she'd actually believed he'd discovered her deception...and accepted it. For a few strange precious moments the weight of her secret had been lifted, and she could merely be a woman passionate about marine life speaking with a man she desired.

Her burden, the one she'd voluntarily subjugated herself toward, remained.

At least she hadn't revealed her secret. The captain's jovial humor would certainly halt if she confessed her deception. The man hadn't even liked having her on board his ship yesterday, and that had been with a servant.

Though she trusted him not to take advantage of her female form were he to discover she was merely in disguise, it would not do for word to spread on the ship that a woman was on board. She had no desire for a hoard of roughened sailors to discover she was the only female within hundreds of miles.

Despite the captain's earlier dismissive demeanor, he was not entirely without some good qualities. In fact, he seemed in possession of very many good qualities.

Good qualities that it would bequeath her to ignore, lest she find herself laughing too hard at his jokes or find her eyes softening too much when he grew more serious. Nor would it be advisable for her attention to linger on the broadness of his chest, the pleasing curve of his neck, and the brightness of his eyes.

Resisting that temptation seemed more insurmountable than even conducting her research.

She would strive to not do anything to subject herself further to his suspicions.

On this ship, she was a man. That's all the captain needed to know, despite the strange urge she had to tell him everything about her life.

"So what is your impression of us English? Besides being terrible, of course." Captain Rosse's deep voice filled the room, and his lips curved in a roguish grin that seemed to have a direct link to the pattering of her heart.

The captain moved to fetch more rum, and his dark, polished boots gleamed under the candlelight. His breeches curved in a sinful manner over sinewy thighs. The masculine scent of cedar and rum pervaded the room, and the dark furniture, swathed in shadows, varied so much from the spacious, light parlor rooms to which she was accustomed.

She took another sip of rum, but the alcohol still burned her throat, and she still coughed.

The captain smiled. "I suppose you're not used to the Caribbean variety."

"Oh. Yes. Suppose I should have taken the brandy," she lied.

She hoped brandy did not have a similar burn.

Captain Rosse remained silent.

She needed to think of something apart from the broadness of the man's shoulders. Or the succulent curve of his lips. Or his knowing sultry gaze.

It didn't matter if his features were perfectly symmetrical, or if his tousled hair gleamed in the candlelight. It didn't matter if his masculine scent wafted over her, and it certainly didn't matter that the hint of sweat and sandalwood seemed the most impressive thing in the world.

It didn't matter because she was a man.

"So how did you find England?" the captain asked.

She could have kissed him for making her think of something else.

Hmph.

Now she was contemplating kissing him. And even though she'd never kissed anyone before, the thought of kissing him inundated her mind. If only she'd never read her stepsister's books.

She sighed, and her heart fluttered.

"I enjoyed my visit," she said.

Mostly.

Her voice may have squeaked, and she took care to cough. She stretched her legs and crossed her arms over her chest in the authoritative manner that all men seemed to hold, even though if a woman had done it—if she had done it, her mother and governess and both sisters would only scold her.

She took another sip of rum, and this time she prepared herself for the already familiar burn. "The countryside looked beautiful."

"Much tamer than your undeveloped woods and fields."

"Yes." She pressed her lips together. She considered herself intelligent, but she seemed to have displaced her normally extensive vocabulary in favor of a smattering of positive, enthusiastic words that she didn't know if she should attribute to the English countryside or to the captain himself.

He was beautiful.

Most definitely.

"And the people? How do you find us English?" Even though he was only a captain, his accent seemed refined, and she fought the urge to sigh and say they were the most amazing people in the world. The temptation was strong—ridiculously strong, but it wouldn't be correct.

She'd enjoyed spending time with Lady Rockport, even though the marchioness had seemed cold when they'd first met.

Similarly, she'd enjoyed spending time with Fiona, her brother's bride, though she'd anticipated enjoying her company. She and Percival shared the same parents, and their similar taste couldn't be shocking.

But the rest of the English? Apart from the ones whose company had been meticulously selected by her brothers?

She sighed, recollecting the extent to which she'd attempted to meet her family's demands, and how openly and painfully she'd failed. She'd mastered the etiquette and dance steps. She'd practiced pianoforte so to best entertain gentlemen at house parties, training her fingers to fly over the black and white keys to the unfamiliar imperialistic British songs. Yet it had never mattered.

Every potential suitor simply saw her as an American. After word spread of her interest in marine life, they'd been eager to demean her further, asking her questions, and then rather than lauding her ability to answer them, they declared her a bluestocking of the very worst sort. When had knowledge become a thing to despise?

No, she was glad to be outside Britain's borders, no matter how striking the white chalk cliffs that lined the country, or how impressive the brick and limestone manor homes scattered about the hills and dales.

"What did you do in England?" Captain Rosse asked.

"I attended some balls. Some house parties."

"As a scientist?" The captain raised his eyebrows.

She squirmed and imbibed more rum. She focused on the warm taste, and not on the quickening pace of her heart. "Just a few balls."

She'd gone to every single one. Every single major one that season, and nothing, absolutely nothing had happened.

She closed her eyes. She didn't want to relive the humiliation of discovering that the English, even though they'd acted pleasant to her, had been laughing the whole time. She didn't want to remember that dreadful article in *Matchmaking for Wallflowers*.

Goodness.

If that gleefully malevolent article had never been published, then Sir Seymour would never have read it and would never have rushed to Brighton with his unmarried son. He would never have been able to convince her mother that his son was Louisa's only option to ease her humiliation.

If only she'd been somewhat prettier. If only she had disguised her intelligence, feigning interest in horse racing and fox hunting as the other debutantes did.

"To be honest," she admitted, "I did not find the English overly pleasant. Perhaps the more regular ones are fine—but the upper-class people, they were dreadful. The *ton*. I'm proud that my neighbors in Massachusetts fought to leave Britain."

"A true American."

She beamed. "Yes."

"Though surely you couldn't have had much to do with the *ton*?" His gaze dropped to her wrinkled breeches, and she placed her hands on her lap, conscious of the plain fabric. Heat rushed to her cheeks, and she glanced at the crystal tumbler. The amber-colored liquid had decreased.

She'd been more forthcoming than she'd intended.

She didn't reach for the rum this time.

She couldn't trust what would happen if she did.

"Forgive me," she said. "I shouldn't insult the *ton*. You're English. You may be friends with—"

"I'm just nobody," Captain Rosse interrupted. "Not important at all."

His fists tightened, and her heart seemed to constrict at a similarly unwanted rate.

"Perhaps I should retire," she said.

He nodded. "Until tomorrow."

"Yes," she said.

She tried to walk with the assertive swagger of a man, but the rolling waves beneath the ship and the rum made any attempt at walking difficult.

The captain smiled. "We're far from England's coast now. This is the open ocean."

She nodded, and then the captain wrapped his arm around her waist. His strength stabilized her, and she smiled at him, distracted by the scent of sweat and seaspray. She strove not to lean into him. She strove not to appear as if it were anything unusual at all to be striding so near a specimen of such undeniable masculinity.

And he wasn't just handsome.

He was kind and entertaining.

He was intelligent—one didn't become a captain if one wasn't comfortable guiding his crew on this expensive concoction of wood and sails and ropes though storm and battle. The man was responsible for keeping it on course and managing the crew.

She considered Sir Seymour and the pride he'd shown in having a son who didn't need to work. She admired Captain Rosse far more, and not despite his occupation.

She sank deeper into the captain's arms, and a warm chuckle sounded in her ear. "Don't fall asleep on me."

She tried not to moan. She thought she'd managed to be silent, but he laughed. *Fiddle-faddle.*

A click sounded, and the door to her cabin swung open.

The captain ambled with her to the small bed. "You're the most lightweight person I've ever seen."

Her cheeks flamed, but she felt him slide her into the bed.

"Oh," she murmured, blissfully. "You probably like scientists then." She had the impression that she might be slurring her words, but if the captain found fault, he didn't say.

"I do like scientists. Especially intelligent ones."

Her eyes shot open, but the door closed, and she was alone. In a new room. On an actual ship. Very, very far from home.

Chapter
Thirteen

Rupert may never have considered himself prone to excessive amounts of smiling, but his lips seemed to veer permanently upward, as if they'd found a gravitational pull toward the sky.

Or Mr. Thornton.

He shook his head. He hadn't thought of himself as lonely, but last night had amused him. *Fish.* Who studied fish? He smiled.

Mr. Thornton didn't resemble the type of passenger to the West Indies he'd expected. He hadn't once confided in Rupert his desire to make his fortune and to build a home in England that rivaled that of the other West Indian sugar tycoons, and he hadn't disparaged those who did not express similar monetary and landowning ambition. He certainly hadn't lamented the rising cost of slaves as more than one distinctly unpleasant landowner had in one of Barbados's public houses.

No, Mr. Thornton was downright agreeable, even

though the man was American. Rupert had braced himself for the typical smugness ex-colonialists tended to feel when faced with an Englishman, spouting sentiments about freedom and independence, when everyone knew that the English had simply not seen the colonies valuable enough to put up a proper fight for.

They'd never have let their sugar plantations in the West Indies go.

Rupert smiled. He already couldn't wait for when they would have dinner later tonight.

Mr. Thornton had dragged a chair from his cabin and placed it on the quarterdeck. He seemed not to care that foamy water from waves slopped onto the vessel's surface with regularity. He gazed at the horizon with an unabashed joy that made something in Rupert's chest ache.

Thornton clutched a notebook, and his hand flew as he sketched the waves. He resembled no one Rupert had ever encountered.

The Americans he'd met had been brash and burly, eager to flaunt their successes in the past wars. The few scientists he'd encountered had been pale-faced fellows who blinked uncertainly, as if surprised to see the sun. And though he couldn't deny Thornton's definite awkwardness, or how at certain moments he'd caught the man jerking his head away from him, as if unpleased to see him, he'd never met a scientist who expressed such passion for his field.

"Didn't know you whistled." Fergus's voice broke through his contemplation. "What do you think about the new passenger?"

Rupert jumped. "You startled me."

"Oh." Fergus chuckled. "Never done that before. Usually you're always so quick, Cap'n."

"Maybe I'm catching a cold," Rupert said, and he averted his head before he could catch Fergus scrutinizing him again.

Or remarking that Rupert didn't appear to have the least bit of a cold.

"If I'd known you had a passion for whistling, Cap'n, I would 'ave suggested you join us when we all play together. Better than Ole Jeremiah's singing, that's for bloody sure."

"I don't have a passion for it," Rupert insisted.

"Ah, just break into spontaneous song? Rather romantic like." Fergus smirked.

"I'm not—" Rupert halted his bluster as Fergus's smirk widened. His cheeks heated, even though, with this wind, he shouldn't be feeling the least bit warm. "Never mind."

The words were a faint rebuke, and Fergus's smile did not disappear.

Fergus remained beside him, and Rupert tore his hand through his hair.

"The scientist is a good passenger. Quiet," Rupert said, addressing Fergus's initial question.

"Didn't seem quiet last night," Fergus said. "Think I couldn't hear you too laughing then?"

"I—"

"Don't think I've seen you so content since you've been with a woman."

Rupert grunted. "You're not supposed to speak to your superior in such terms."

Fergus shrugged.

The man was silent, Lord bless him, but his words had already made him think far too much.

He scrunched his fingers around the rail of the ship, and the breeze rippled over him.

Perhaps... He shifted his legs over the deck, conscious of the sailors' occasional questioning glances at him.

There was something strange about the scientist. Something almost *fascinating*. He frowned.

He'd never attributed a man with that particular quality before. Intelligence, perhaps. Confidence, certainly. But not being...fascinating.

He found his gaze drifting toward the scientist again. Thornton was consumed with his sketches. It might only be the waves now, but he knew the man would draw fish when they reached the Caribbean. He'd explained how his diving helmet functioned, though when Rupert had suggested he demonstrate it before him, he'd only blushed.

Was it possible he made him uncomfortable?

Rupert almost laughed.

He certainly hadn't meant to intimidate Mr. Thornton. Unless...

He blinked.

There *was* something about how the light struck Mr. Thornton's cheeks... Something about how Thornton tilted up his head, as if to wonder at the height of the masts that made Rupert desire to tousle his hair. It was the sort of gesture that the company of a woman might inspire in him.

Last night they'd been in a dark room, but now his appearance was clearly exposed. His body was slender, perhaps explained by the man's inclination to study books rather than the hard labor the sailors took on.

The man's hair, tied back almost too harshly, seemed to highlight his cheeks more. Or at least he seemed to be spending an inordinate amount of time musing about his heart-shaped face.

He appeared almost...feminine.

A fact that should have been a disagreeable quality, at least in a man, and yet Rupert was most certainly not thinking unflattering thoughts.

He knew Mr. Thornton's sister had brought the diving helmet on the ship, but in the stark light of the sun, the resemblance seemed even more pronounced.

He hadn't noticed it in the dim light below deck, but his skin looked like it didn't even need to see a razor.

Odd.

Distinctly, definitely odd.

Unless... Thornton had small, dainty hands. He recalled the moments last night his laughter had rung with a higher pitch quality like that of a boy whose voice hadn't shifted. The man looked young, but he'd certainly advanced past voice changing age.

He wanted to laugh. The woman who'd brought the diving helmet couldn't possibly have disguised herself, could she have?

He stared at the scientist again. He wished he'd paid more attention in Brighton.

"I should see to the passenger," Rupert said, moving from Fergus.

It wasn't possible.

Mr. Thornton couldn't be a woman.

The thought was ridiculous, confined to hallucinations better explained to thirsty men in the desert.

And yet...

He marched toward the scientist. "May I speak to you in private?"

Mr. Thornton—or whoever this person was—raised his eyebrows.

Rupert noted they were thinner than the bushy brows that adorned the sailors, though the scientist would not be the first man to pay attention to his appearance. Rupert may not have attended a ball amongst the *ton* in years, but he'd not entirely lost all memories of those lavish, overtly sumptuous occasions. The men in those festivities had been attired in enough velvet and satin to rival any woman, and the cut of their pantaloons had revealed the shape of their legs, ostensibly to best show their mastery of the complex dance steps.

Rupert frowned. He'd never found those men appealing and had greatly favored mingling with the women, lingering on full bosoms and luscious locks when he had the chance.

Blast.

If he'd been tricked.

He'd been a pirate captain. He'd tricked enemy ships. He'd been sneaky and cunning... If some chit had lied her way on board, even when it was expressly forbidden to travel alone—

He shook his head.

He better not have been fooled.

On the other hand—what woman would be foolish enough to venture onto a ship on her own? Especially one bound for the West Indies, of all the dangerous places in the world to choose?

"You haven't been honest with me," Rupert said, and the scientist's eyes flickered to his side. Rupert knew guilty men. He'd met enough of them. One didn't become a captain without being able to note when a sailor was lapsing on his duties.

"What do you mean?" Mr. Thornton's voice wobbled, and he flushed.

Rupert refused to contemplate the adorableness of the rosy shade adorning the man's cheeks, and he firmed his jaw. "Below deck, now."

The scientist widened his eyes, and he jumped up. His books and papers remained piled on the deck, and vibrant illustrations lay beside duller, carefully inscribed notes.

"You, er, should probably take your things with you. I wouldn't want a gust to blow them into the ocean."

The man nodded and picked up his papers. Rupert peered over the man's shoulder, noting impeccably drawn waves. With a few strokes he had seemed to encapsulate the setting perfectly.

He frowned. He was supposed to be interrogating him. Not admiring his artistic prowess.

"Follow me," Rupert said, his voice gruff, and he headed toward his quarters, relieved to hear scampering behind him.

He descended the steep steps, marched through the corridor, ducking his head, and pushed open the door to his quarters. The table had long been cleared, and he cringed at the memory of their evening together.

He'd confided too much. He tilted his head at Mr. Thornton. *Miss Thornton?*

"How can I help you?" Thornton's voice wobbled, and for some absurd reason, the fact made his heart squeeze.

"You tell me." He firmed his jaw and stared into wide-set gray eyes. "I don't believe you are who you say you are."

He stared at Thornton's cheeks. They appeared...soft. Not scruffy like all the other men's after they'd scraped a razor against them. His cheeks looked smooth, almost feminine, and he placed his hand on them.

*

Anger glinted from Captain Rosse's eyes. His nostrils flared, and Louisa's heartbeat ratcheted. The man's hand remained on her face, sending an unwelcome heat surging through her.

"Put your hand down," she ordered, but the man's hand scarcely wavered.

"You've been lying to me," he said.

She stepped back, and her spine slammed against the wooden wall. The captain narrowed the distance between them, and his clear blue eyes sparked with anger.

This wasn't good.

He's found me out.

She couldn't let this happen. She couldn't be discovered. She couldn't admit she was a woman on board a ship filled with men. She couldn't give up the possibility of doing research.

"You're a woman," the captain said.

She struggled from his grip, but his hold tightened around her waist.

Dread filled her.

How did he know? She'd attempted to be so careful.

He's only suspicious.

And she refused to confirm his suspicion.

She widened her eyes carefully and took care to keep her pitch low. "Nonsense!"

He smiled, as if he'd expected her to protest.

Her mind scampered and skipped, desperate to think of something— anything—to keep him from confirming his suspicions.

"It's true." Her throat seemed to think she'd stepped

into the Sahara instead of his quarters, and she struggled
to speak, but she forced herself to continue. "I'm not who
I said I was."

He gave a short, harsh laugh. "I believe you."

"I'm—not a scholar." She refused the inclination to
rest her gaze anywhere but on him and his darkening eyes.

He blinked, and she carried forward, heartened by his
hesitancy.

"I lied about...that."

"Oh."

She forced herself to laugh. "I am too young, but I
wanted validation."

"Oh." He stared at her again.

"I would hope that you wouldn't tell anyone..." She
attempted to smile. "But I'm certainly not a woman. I
mean..." she laughed, hoping the wobble was not as
apparent to him as it sounded to her, "...that would be
ridiculous."

"I don't believe you," he growled.

His gaze dropped to her chest, and a wild idea occurred
to her.

Her heart rate hammered, but she had to convince
him. Her bosom was always meager, but now it was bound.
She grabbed his hand, ignoring the sharp heat that jolted
through her at meeting his skin. His eyes widened for a
moment, and she ignored the desire to gaze into them.

Instead she jerked his hand to her chest and placed
it against her flattened bosom. Sun-kissed skin touched
where no man had ever touched, and her legs weakened
beneath her. The wooden wall pressed against her as his
firm hand explored her.

The binding was tight.

She was safe.

The captain's confident expression gave way to confusion. "You're not—"

She raised her chin. "Naturally not! That would be utter nonsense."

"But your face—" He swallowed hard. "I mean your skin, your demeanor—"

"I haven't even been to university. I'm too *young*. So please remove your hand from my chest." She tilted her head and allowed her lips to scrunch into one of those dreadful smirks other debutantes made. "Unless you're one of those men who enjoys doing such things?"

"What?" The captain jerked his hand away, and his shoulders slumped down. "Of—of course not."

His cheeks were a definite darker shade than they'd been before.

"Good." She smiled tightly. "I would rather you refrain from any urge to touch my length either."

The captain's eyes widened, and she gestured to her breeches, and the space inside which she'd sewn a masculine appendage.

"Forgive me." The captain stepped backward between them, and she sighed, relieved he'd refrained from groping her there too. The fabric she'd sewn there might be rather less convincing to a man familiar with its appropriate anatomy.

"If I were a woman," she said, "my sister, as you say, I would not have introduced myself to you as a woman first."

"I suppose not," he admitted. "Who are you?"

"Mr. Thornton," she said. "Mr. Sebastian Thornton. Now," Louisa said, eager to leave him, "I should return to my research. You have a ship to captain and not a passenger to grope."

His cheeks reddened further, and she brushed by him quickly before she could make further eye contact.

*

The table was set.

For two people.

Rupert frowned at the place setting. He wasn't prepared to see Thornton again. Perhaps the scientist had inflated his accomplishments, but though that might be a crime in academic circles, it wasn't one on this ship. His lips twisted. Rupert knew more about misrepresenting backgrounds than anyone. Just because he lied about his past, did not mean every person who wandered onto his ship did.

His cheeks still burned at the afternoon's incident. He'd spent the whole morning looking forward to dining with Mr. Thornton again, and now he desired nothing so much as to avoid him.

Where was a ferocious storm when he needed one?

He'd humiliated himself. Groping the man's chest. What woman in her right mind would possibly disguise herself as a man and board a ship filled with men headed toward the West Indies?

Not a bloody single one.

Women's sensibilities excluded the potential for such outrageous actions.

He sucked in a deep breath of air. If he could face Americans in the midst of war, if he could attack French ships and steal their loot for his country, he could certainly face the scientist.

Theoretically.

Even if he had a very clear memory of nearly tearing

off the man's shirt, and even if he'd almost thought he'd felt something more on the man's chest. That had been fantasy. A mere glimpse at the man's breeches had revealed that.

"Captain Rosse?" Thornton's voice interrupted his musings.

"Forgive me. I did not hear you enter." Rupert forced himself to smile.

The gesture did not seem to assure Thornton. He still hadn't met his eyes. Likely Thornton was terrified Rupert would force himself on him again, shoving him against the wall, and—

Heat burned Rupert's cheeks again.

"I don't have to eat—"

Blast.

The man's discomfort could almost be described as adorable. Rupert's smile came more naturally this time. "I'm sure you have to eat."

"I mean—I needn't eat here." He looked downward, and Rupert was struck by the length of the man's sooty lashes. *Double blast.*

"Nonsense." Rupert settled into his chair, more for his benefit than Thornton's. He gestured to the seat opposite him.

Thornton sat down gingerly, as if worried Rupert might decide to accost him again.

Rupert forced himself to focus on his food and not the manner in which the candlelight flickered over Thornton's face.

He scowled. He'd been so certain Thornton was a woman. Something in his chest tightened. *Disappointment?*

"So tell me about your deception," Rupert said finally.

Thornton widened his eyes, and his hands shook as he tore a piece of bread.

"Overstating your scientific background," Rupert prompted.

Thornton seemed to exhale. "I shouldn't have done it."

"Then why did you?" Rupert asked

He hesitated. "I thought it might help me get a place on the ship."

Rupert chuckled, and the tension in his body eased. "We're not very elitist here. You didn't need to worry about that at all."

Thornton's uncertain smile widened. "It just seemed like such a dream. Visiting the West Indies."

"I'll have to show you around," Rupert said, and he grinned as the man's face pinkened, and his eyelashes swooped downward.

*

Louisa had expected the worst when she'd been ushered to the captain's quarters again. She would never forget the memory of his hands on her wrists, his breath against his ear, and his eyes roaming over her.

His eyes now seemed determined to look anywhere but her.

"When was the first time you visited the West Indies," she said, eager to discuss anything, absolutely anything except the matter on which they were no doubt both dwelling.

"I joined the Royal Navy ten years ago."

"Ah. So you remember when we defeated you at sea."

"You know," the captain mused, "I could remove that food from your plate after all."

She smiled. "In all fairness, we never expected to defeat you."

"I'm not confident you did. Some of your generals were appalling."

"Perhaps in parts of the country. Near Canada. Not on the ocean."

"So after spending your youth laughing at the British when reading about us in the broadsheets, you decided to actually visit Britain?"

She smiled. "Clearly I'm in need of continued amusement."

He flushed again and took a deep sip of wine. Perhaps the man was thinking of his actions today, and her heart squeezed. She wished she could ease his embarrassment and tell him that all his suspicions had been utterly correct.

"What really brought you there?" The captain asked.

She hesitated. She couldn't tell him it had been to find a husband.

"I would have thought you might have booked a voyage to the West Indies sooner," the captain added. "Surely the fish in England cannot differ so greatly from those in Massachusetts. Or are there great examples of marine life native to England of which I'm unaware?"

"You don't seem to have much faith in the appeal of your home country, Captain Rosse."

"Actually I had a pleasant experience there recently," he mused. "I hope to return soon."

They spoke longer, and the uneasy rhythm of her heartbeat steadied, and she found the intervals between her smiles narrowing.

Chapter
Fourteen

Wind blustered over Rupert, and the ship dipped up and down. Foamy waves crested against the hull, and sharp gusts swallowed the sailors' shouts.

The air was warmer, and the sea was crisper, clearer. The weeks had passed far too quickly, and soon they would be in Barbados. Sailors rushed about, eager to be docked, and he spoke with them and ascertained the course.

Rupert was painfully aware of Thornton. Though he prided himself on knowing what was happening above deck, he was certain so much time should not be spent on reflecting on the scientist's every move. Each arch of the man's neck to more closely observe the dolphins that leaped from the ocean seemed to send a tinge of longing through every single one of his nerves.

He descended the narrow staircase and returned to his quarters. Had he developed some form of strange obsession? Perhaps derived from being so long at sea?

Blast. Had he forgotten what true women looked like? Or was he so desperate for them that he optimistically investigated under the attire of men?

He settled onto his chair and removed his ledger. Images of the scientist floated through his mind instead of the rows of black digits before him. He shifted his body against the hard wooden back of the chair.

Clearly he needed to see some women, actual women, not simply men whose slender features made him contemplate...

More images, naughtier images, dashed through his mind.

The man's soft skin, perhaps simply a testament to his youth and family traits, seemed to shine in his mind, and on more than one occasion he'd fought the urge to brush his fingers over the sumptuous smoothness. He wanted to delve his fingers in the man's locks, and he yearned to trace his fingers over the scientist's chiseled features, and perhaps unravel his always appallingly tied cravat.

Rupert had always enjoyed kissing necks.

Energy surged through him, and he sprang up from his seat. The cabin was too narrow, too constricting, and it was too tempting to consider—

Bloody hell.

He slammed his hand against the wall, as if the jolt of pain might tumble the thoughts from his mind.

His nostrils flared, and he marched back upstairs. He craved distraction.

He inhaled the salty air eagerly when he reentered the deck. He avoided the gazes of the sailors, as if they might be able to ascertain his innermost thoughts.

By God, he needed a woman.

He needed some normalcy.

He reminded himself that he was happy. This was why he didn't return to England. This was why he didn't seek a wife and promptly attempt to sire an heir and spares with the vigor suited to a future duke.

But the strange energy continued to surge through him, and he continued to pace the deck.

A ship's environment was inherently unnatural—a fact of which Rupert had never been so painfully aware. Likely Thornton also missed the company of women.

Sadness surged through him, and Rupert shook his head. He never felt sad. That was an emotion to befall others, with less steely control of their spirits.

Rupert vowed to at least show Mr. Thornton a good time. That was the very least he could do. And on the island...Rupert smiled. He knew exactly where he would take him.

*

When Louisa had last been in the Americas, the leaves had already been in their final death throes. The tree colors were murky, and more leaves had adorned the ground than branches. Even the grass had paled, and the once vibrant wildflowers had died, their stiff corpses waving awkwardly in the wind.

No such fate had befallen the nature here. Perhaps later in the year, the clouds would become gray, and the flowers would disappear. Not now.

Palm trees dotted the coast. Their leaves, longer than any she was accustomed to fanned in the soft breeze. The turquoise water sparkled under the strong sunbeams, but the vibrant trees and bushes managed to equal the intensity of the beauty.

Her eyes sparkled. "We're almost there."

The ship neared the port. They would stay on this island for one week, before heading to Jamaica, where she would be able to find Arthur. Her brother would be able to arrange transport home for her, though hopefully she might stay with him longer and do more research.

She sighed. The thought of seeing Arthur again should have brought her joy, and she told herself that it still did, but she also couldn't shake the sorrow that she would need to leave Captain Rosse. *The Sapphire Princess* already felt like more of a home to her than any actual home ever had.

Tomorrow morning she would sneak off the ship to do her research. Only a few more hours to go... And then she would be swimming. Underwater. With all the fish she'd always dreamed of seeing.

The sun beat down on her, and she sighed in the pleasant warmth. Her secret remained undiscovered.

She would get away with this.

She tried to shake the feeling of guilt at her family's inevitable bewilderment when they'd discovered her missing.

"I may have a surprise for you." Captain Rosse beamed down at her.

"Indeed? You did not need to do that." Her eyes softened as she gazed at him, wondering at how he managed to appear so wonderful and remain so considerate, and he looked away hastily.

He stretched his hand to his collar and moved his gaze toward the horizon. A pale, ever so enticing strip of sand separated the palm trees from the turquoise water. Likely Captain Rosse's eagerness to land equaled hers.

"You should dress nicely tonight," he said.

"Are we in such good company?" Something in Louisa's heart tightened. It wasn't proper for him to hold such an effect over her.

Captain Rosse smiled secretively. "Good is not the proper word."

Her lips spread into a similar smile, and joy surged through her. His happiness was the dearest thing to her. She peered up at him. Sunbeams shone over him, highlighting every golden lock of his hair.

She could think of myriad *not good* things about him.

It would be nice to imagine that he desired to stroll the seashore with her and watch the sunset with her at his side.

His eyes continued to twinkle, and her cheeks warmed, and she averted her gaze, her heartbeat thundering at the thought of tonight.

Chapter Fifteen

The sun toppled downward, and the sky turned orange. The verdant leaves that crowned each tree darkened into a shade that most resembled ebony. Pink and lilac light dabbled over the clouds, moving over the once azure sky. Captain Rosse managed to be once again thoroughly correct, Louisa mused.

Good certainly was not the proper word.

He'd taken her to a brothel.

Or at least that's what Louisa assumed from the abundant collection of scantily clad women and the unmistakable sounds of moaning coming from the huts.

The leaves continued to flutter in the breeze, but the landscape had transformed, and the scent of incense and spices seemed to thicken in the already heavy air, as if no longer emboldened to compete with the once colorful scenery. Torches flickered on the beach. Dark-skinned women reclined on chairs, swathed in jeweled fabrics.

"This way." He strolled toward the brothel.

Louisa's feet sank into the soft sand, and she struggled

to follow him with equal force, even if she was certain she wanted to be nowhere near such an establishment.

Stars sparkled from the sky, but no man admired the heavens at this time. Other sailors from their ship, and other white-skinned men, mingled with the dark-skinned women. She turned to Rupert. He must be embarrassed that they'd happened upon such an unsavory location.

But no embarrassment flickered over the captain's face. "I thought you might enjoy this."

"Oh?" Louisa's voice squeaked, and she coughed furiously. "This is...the surprise?"

Goodness.

She'd hoped for something else. He had sent her knowing looks, and for some ridiculous reason she'd believed...

She'd been an absolute fool to imagine there might be another reason he desired her company. He might eat with her at dinner, on those nights when the sea was calm and his presence was not required above deck, but the first time they set foot on actual land, he ushered her to such a disreputable establishment.

"I thought you must tire of our discussions in my quarters." Captain Rosse laughed, but the laugh sounded forced and almost...pained.

She swallowed hard.

"I could never tire of them," she said solemnly.

"Oh?"

She nodded, not avoiding his gaze, even though she knew she should.

Rupert flushed. "We've been at sea a long time. I thought you might appreciate a diversion."

There was a trace of uncertainty in his voice, and Louisa reminded herself that there was no need to ponder the reason. It was likely something to do with sailing or some past experience.

Not her.

Certainly not her.

A man who brought his friend to a harem of women did not possess any feelings toward his friend. These women, with their curved bodies glinting with jewels and exotic fabrics, did not resemble a pale, thin New England scientist.

Her stomach tightened, but she strove to retain a cheerful demeanor. "This is marvelous. A wonderful surprise."

"You like it?" His voice wobbled, and she nodded vehemently. She did not want him to think she had any inappropriate affection for him herself.

"Naturally," she said airily. "They are beautiful women."

"Ah, yes," the captain said.

"The sailors seem quite happy with them," she said. "Er—good sign."

"Indeed."

Someone was beating drums, and the already humid air seemed to thicken. The women's attire revealed most everything, and she forced her gaze away from splaying hips and generous bosoms.

She shivered. Was this what men desired? Certainly those women with whom the sailors joyfully met could not vary more from her—even when she was attired in the traditional female manner.

"They're not wearing very much," she said before her cheeks warmed. She coughed. "It's, er, good to see. *Naturally.*"

The captain nodded. "I thought you would like it."

She smiled tightly.

She didn't like it.

She absolutely didn't like it, but she tried to imitate some of the lustful gazes actual men might give in this situation. Certainly there were enough men about expressing their delight at the situation to imitate.

"Quite different from women up in New England," she said, trying to sound authoritative, and realizing too late that authoritative might not be the right note expected. "I mean—their ankles are on display."

"Quite more than their ankles," the captain responded, and humor tinged his voice.

This was how she liked him to be. Happy and joyful.

Yet she did not want that joy to be caused by the half-nude women splayed over the beach.

"You may have a point." She cast another glance at the women. "Er—awfully good."

She shivered. The women couldn't resemble her less. She despised the cloth she'd wrapped tightly around her bosom to bind it. She despised her breeches and shirt. She despised that she'd worn her boots, which made her gait—never very elegant—even clumsier as they sank into the sand. She even despised the heat and how it caused the back of her neck to prickle and sweat to slide down her brow.

Though perhaps it was unfair to entirely blame the heat.

Her foolish expectations and the captain's forceful delight at his location seemed more at fault.

"Are you fine?" Concern sounded in Captain Rosse's tone, and her heart ached. He'd been sweet—in a fashion.

"Splendid." She used her deepest voice and attempted

to conjure something like delight. She paused and then rubbed her hands together. "I, er, just want to grab them."

"Oh. Me too. Er—naturally. I—I didn't know what you would think. But there are some rooms in the back if you would like some privacy." He took a deep breath, and his face contorted into an expression a painter might use when depicting a hero right before he rode to his death. "Which woman would you like?"

"I'll just have a look around. Wouldn't want to get the wrong one, right?" She gave her most confident nod and then laughed.

The captain joined her, though his laugh sounded weaker and more uncomfortable. "Very well."

She had the strangest sensation that she'd given the wrong answer. She'd tried to maintain the illusion she was a man—but was he testing her for another reason?

"I'll meet you at the ship," Captain Rosse said. "Can you find your way back?"

She blinked. She'd rather assumed he'd want to partake in the activities, but instead his face appeared ashen.

She nodded. "Naturally. We men are quite capable of that. Quite an, er, masculine trait."

The captain nodded, tension still visible in his face, and he padded away from her, his shoulders sunk.

She was alone.

With about twenty ladies of the night and even more sailors.

*

He wasn't thinking about the women.

Their cleavage might be displayed, their cheeks might

be rouged and the curve of their hips evident as they sprawled on the beach.

Other sailors sprinted toward them, as if they were the finest sirens.

There was only one person with whom he wanted to spend time. And unfortunately he wanted to do rather more than to spend time with him.

Frustration ratcheted through Rupert, and the ocean lapped in rhythmic waves at odds with the careening of his heart. He sank onto the sand and peered at the dark waves. One person was swimming. *Another thing I don't do.*

This was supposed to be happiness. This was the day his sailors anticipated with eagerness—the first day after crossing the Atlantic they were on solid land.

"Captain Rosse?" Thornton's voice sounded behind him.

"Go to the party," Rupert growled, keeping his gaze on the shoreline. He cursed that his entire body seemed ridiculously aware of the other man's presence. The very hairs on his arms prickled.

"You overestimate my passion for brothels," Thornton said.

"Even for the finest women in the Caribbean?"

"Somehow I doubt that. Though even if that were the case..." Thornton didn't finish the thought, and a strange disappointment surged through Rupert.

Thornton settled beside him and glided his hands through the delicate sand. "I never thought I'd be able to experience this."

"Mm-hmm."

The man stretched his arms over his head, perhaps to remain lackadaisical, but Rupert's gaze was directed at his chest and the manner in which his attire tightened around it.

He cursed the flickering lights of the lanterns, and his throat dried, as if the only thing his blasted body was capable of doing was regarding the scientist. The memory of pressing his hand against Thornton's chest seemed to soar through him.

"Why didn't you like the entertainment?" Rupert hadn't meant for his voice to quiver, and he coughed. "Do your...tastes differ from that of other men?"

Thornton gave an awkward laugh. "Perhaps you are correct that I do not have much in common with the other sailors."

Hope for something he did not understand rose through Rupert. Were the pinkening of cheeks, the tucking of hair behind his ear, the sudden averting of his gaze away from him important? Could that indicate...interest?

He'd never experienced such a thing before. He'd always been more than happy to bed women. Had never desired, or even contemplated, doing the same with a man. Perhaps stopping being a pirate had softened him.

Tension rose in him, and he was too aware of Thornton's slender feet stretched before him, and the manner in which his breeches hugged his slender thighs.

He gritted his teeth and stared straight before him. It didn't matter that the man smelled vaguely of vanilla. It didn't matter that he felt some strange urge to pull him toward him.

He glanced at Thornton's face, and the scientist's lips were pulled into a brave expression.

Thornton's small hand lay on the sand.

It felt warm and soft below his fingers.

He blinked.

Had he clasped onto Thornton's hand? But there it was beneath his. Softer and smoother and more enticing than any man's hand had a right to be.

A sharp intake of breath sounded beside him, and his cheeks heated. In the next moment Thornton moved his hand from beneath his, and Rupert shivered at the lack of contact between them.

"Compared to the sailors," Thornton said, "I may be more...academically inclined."

Oh.

Simply because Thornton possessed too much honor to indulge in the island's famed vices did not mean he cast aside the whole fairer sex.

Rupert's cheeks flamed.

"I should go. I—I have research in the morning." Thornton gave a stiff wave in Rupert's direction, not quite meeting his eyes, and hurried away.

Chapter Sixteen

Louisa slipped from her narrow bed. The ship barely moved in the water, a reminder that they were anchored. She might finally use her diving helmet in the Caribbean, just as she'd always dreamed.

She glanced in the direction of Captain Rosse's quarters. What had he meant last night?

She remembered the short blissful sensation of his hand over hers, and the vague sense that she should have said more to him last night.

She lifted the diving helmet. She wished she might wear her diving costume, but she could swim in breeches and a shirt. She wouldn't be the first person to do so, even if all the sailors tended to swim shirtless. She dressed quickly and exited the room, clutching the diving helmet.

A creak sounded.

Was it the captain? She hurried down the corridor. She had no desire to speak with him. She had no idea what she would say. Not confiding in him now felt wrong.

She remembered she hadn't put on her binding, but she shook her head. It was for the best. It would take too long for the cloth to dry, and she would need to wear it the rest of the day.

Her heart hammered as she clambered down the ledge of the ship into the turquoise waves. She fastened the long tubes onto the side of the ship and pulled the diving helmet over her head.

The warm water rustled around Louisa, and she dove deeper into the ocean, careful to keep her body vertical. A school of tangerine fish flitted before her, swishing their fins with an elegance she associated more with swaggering *ton* members. Some larger, more independent-minded fish hovered beside the hull, as if hopeful their jeweled coloring might blend into the murky wood beams.

Black striped fish skirted out of her way, skipping merrily over the coral.

She dove deeper, immersing herself into this wonderful new world.

The world she'd never imagined she'd see.

Her heart thudded merrily at the fish before her. Everywhere she looked was glorious.

It should have sufficed.

Yet her mind lingered to the moment last night when the captain had taken her hand in his. Her heart still thundered at the recollection of his large fingers and roughened palm settling over her hand.

She dove deeper, as if the jeweled fish flitting in the aqua waters past her might distract her from the captain.

Splashing sounded above her, and she stilled. Perhaps a dolphin had joined her?

Or a shark? Fish scurried away.

A dark shadow loomed, and the water rippled around it. She glanced at the tubes tied to the ship and swam toward the surface, lest some beast tear the tubes.

No teeth or large eyes confronted her. A boat lumbered through the water. Oars pierced the idyllic haven, and her heartbeat halted as a new rhythm crashed through the gentle ripple of the waves.

She was no longer alone.

She froze as if it were the least bit possible to imagine that the clear water could keep her hidden.

But in the next moment a burly hand grabbed her shoulder and dragged her toward the surface. She kicked her legs, and her heart quickened, as if desperate the extra beats might help her flee.

Unfortunately the arm was strong, the iron hold impossible to evade, and Louisa's head was dragged over the surface.

The turquoise water, the schools of fish, the coral, were replaced with a glaring face, red with obvious rage, and Captain Rosse's blue eyes bored into her.

"Who are you?" Each word seemed to be punctuated with a sneer, and his eyes lingered on her bosom.

She swallowed hard and glanced downward. The white, thin muslin clung to her body indecently, the fabric appearing far too sheer.

She jerked her arm over her torso.

Fiddle-faddle.

Panic swelled through her. She needed to think, needed to say something, but her mouth dried, and air caught in her lungs. She attempted to dive back into the ocean, anything to escape the man's disapproval, but Captain Rosse's arms fastened around her shoulders, and he hauled her over the ledge of the rowboat. Water pooled over the wooden planks, and she scrambled to the seat.

"Answer," he growled.

"Th-Thornton," she stammered.

He laughed, but nothing about the harsh, hollow sound was pleasant.

"You're lying. And pull that contraption off you. *Now.*"

She removed it hastily and hugged the copper concoction, as if the barrier against the ocean might also offer protection against the darkening of the captain's eyes and the fear that surged through her.

"I am Thornton," she repeated. "Sebastian Thornton."

Captain Rosse's expression remained hard and unwavering. "Stop lying."

"You're not even a man." His hand gestured toward her body, toward the manner in which her wet attire clung to her form, highlighting every curve in an indecent manner.

"I—"

But he was right. There were no answers. She'd lied about her identity. She couldn't deny it. She averted her eyes, hating that she couldn't look at him as she admitted that everything she'd ever told him was a fabrication.

"You're right," she admitted softly.

His hand swept over her face, and his fingers traced her features. "What woman disguises herself as a man?"

She yanked her legs toward her, and the boat wobbled beneath her.

He clasped hold of the oars, and his knuckles whitened around the handle. "You should have told me."

"I couldn't." She wasn't certain if the unsteadiness of her body or the relentless lapping of the waves caused the world to tilt.

"Tell me you're not a spy." He growled.

She gave a harsh laugh. "Of course not! Why would I be? We're not even at war!"

"Did my parents hire you?" He jerked his oars, and salt water splashed over the rim of the boat, though they did not succeed in cooling Louisa's warming cheeks or the fire from his eyes.

Louisa tilted her head, uncomfortable under the harsh sunbeams that beat over the captain, crowning him as if he were some wrathful king. "Parents? I thought you were impressed into the navy..."

"Right." The captain stiffened and settled back into his seat. The boat ceased its dangerous rocking. "Who are you then? Why in God's name did you pretend to be a man? Is there even a Mr. Thornton?"

Her shoulders sagged. When she spoke again, her voice was low, and she avoided his gaze. "He couldn't go on the ship. And I—I wanted to do my research. It's *my* diving helmet."

"Idiocy," he muttered, and she flinched. "You could have been killed."

"But my research!"

His expression softened. "You are really just interested in science."

She waited for a continuation of his tirade, but instead he crashed his oars into the foamy sea and rowed them to the ship in large, sweeping movements.

It was odd that he'd chosen a boat to fetch her in—she hadn't swum far from the hull. In the next moment he ushered her onto the ladder and followed her onto *The Sapphire Princess*.

Only a few sailors were on the deck, and she held her diving helmet and compilation of hoses over her bosom. He ushered her downstairs, and her heart thumped, conscious that everything in the new world she so loved had changed. Would the captain throw her off the ship? Would he never speak to her again?

Chapter
Seventeen

Rupert did not throw this woman over his shoulder and march her to his chambers.

That did not mean he did not consider the option.

Hercules himself had not fought a greater battle.

Blast.

Some woman had disguised herself as a scientist and wrangled her way on board, smattering all laws of propriety. She'd stolen away, though unlike other illegal passengers who hid in crooks and crannies, she'd done it with his full knowledge.

He hadn't even realized it. Instead he'd led her to the most dangerous place on the island and practically demanded she display enthusiasm.

The distance to the door of his cabin seemed to be interminable. Not that achieving privacy with her would solve any problems. Not that locking the door behind them would solve the ache in his heart.

He'd liked Thornton. More than he should have. He'd

told him more things than he'd ever told anyone else before. But this woman was a stranger, an intruder.

She hadn't even bothered to confide her gender to him.

The thoughts he'd entertained must have verged so far from hers.

He sought to calm his breath, but his hands fumbled on the doorknob. The woman, this stranger, wavered beside him, even though she'd entered his room many times before.

But then he also tended not to fumble when confronted with a doorknob.

Finally it swung open, and he pulled this counterfeit Thornton into the room. He slammed the door shut, not caring if he woke the whole ship. The door was closed, he was the captain, and no one would think it unusual for the scientist to enter the room.

He blinked at the familiar furniture. The paintings were still fastened to the wall, incognizant that everything had shifted.

Mr. Thornton did not exist.

Mr. Thornton was a woman.

Rupert scrutinized her.

He bloody well better find out what to call her. "Tell me your name."

Her cheeks pinkened. "That might not be wise—"

"None of this is wise," he said impatiently.

"It's—I'm Louisa," she said. "Louisa Carmichael."

Louisa.

He tested the name in his mind and then rolled it softly over his lips. It was a good American name. Respectable. Not the name of a person destined to stride onto ships wearing breeches.

He turned to her, conscious his nostrils were flaring, conscious he might even be shaking, conscious the British reserve he prided himself in seemed entirely nonexistent.

He inhaled and gestured to the sofa. "Sit."

Louisa widened her eyes and settled hastily down.

He sat in the armchair opposite her. "Tell me exactly what you are doing here."

"Research," she said.

She didn't lower her voice this time, and he blinked. He needed to grow accustomed to the higher pitch.

"You ran away to the West Indies to conduct research." He felt like a fool for repeating her words.

"I suppose it must sound insane."

"You suppose correctly," he growled. "I take it you delivered the diving helmet to the ship."

"It was my diving helmet, and there truly was a Mr. Thornton, but he...backed out."

"So you thought disguising yourself was the acceptable option."

She flushed but nodded.

"You've always struck me as a person of particular intelligence. How could you risk your reputation? Your family must be so worried! How could you risk your *family's* reputation?"

She was silent. "My family's reputation is secure."

"No one's reputation is secure." He thought of his father and the man's misdeeds and grimaced. "Why, you would have to be related to a duke!"

She gave an awkward laugh and directed her gaze toward her lap and her fiddling fingers.

Something in her flushed face made his stomach clench. "You're not related to a duke. Your relatives—your well-off English relatives, they couldn't be—"

"I—" She touched her tightly pulled back hair. "Surely it's not important."

"Of course it's important!"

"Well." She moved her hands to her lap and fiddled with her fingers. "The truth is," she paused, and he took an absurd pleasure in the fact that this conversation was difficult for her as well. "The truth is that *technically my brother* Percival is a duke."

"What on earth does *technically* have to do with the very highest of peers?"

Her cheeks pinkened. "It simply means that people address him as "Your Grace.""

"Good God!"

She shrugged. "Accidental really. Our cousin happened to die, and Percival inherited. Mama packed me off to England to find a husband." Her look became more unsettled.

"And you found one."

"Indeed," she said primly.

"And then abandoned all your duties to flee to the West Indies."

She sighed. "I didn't intend to go. I mean, I dreamed of going, but I never expected to be able to go."

"No one was forcing you."

"My research was on this ship. When Mr. Thornton turned out to have misrepresented himself, I decided to take his place."

"You risked your life."

"This was more important." She untied her hair from that ridiculously harsh queue, and her locks tumbled downward in a decidedly feminine fashion. How had he ever imagined her to be a man before? His fingers itched to brush against the contours of her face.

"Hogwash. Your safety is more important than any notebooks." He smiled despite himself. "But I admire your spirit."

She stared at him, her gray eyes so beautiful, and something like hope stirred in his chest, despite her flagrant betrayal.

"How do you intend to return?" he asked.

"My other brother is in Falmouth, and I wanted to join him."

He sighed. "I'll take you to him when we arrive."

"Thank you." Worry had barely shifted from her face, and something she'd said earlier occurred to him.

"Your last name is *Carmichael?*"

She nodded.

Blast.

"You're one of Arthur Carmichael's sisters," he said miserably.

"You know him?"

He averted his gaze. "I've conducted business with him."

Perhaps the word business might encompass all the things Arthur meant to him. There was no man he'd trusted more than Arthur, and finding someone to trust was most important when he'd worked as a privateer. Somebody needed to handle the goods Rupert had obtained and deliver them to the crown. Somebody needed to authorize his moves. Neither of them wanted Rupert to attack a ship from one of Britain's allies, no matter what treasures might lurk in the locked and bolted hold.

Louisa tilted her head. "I never knew my brother worked. He always gave the impression that he just flitted about and enjoyed a pleasurable life."

Rupert sighed. Arthur belonged to the honorable sort who wouldn't want his family to worry, and knowledge of his occupation would certainly compel them to do so. *Blast.* How on earth had he managed to have Arthur Carmichael's sister on board?

His sister had told him that she'd recommended Mr. Thornton take *The Sapphire Princess.* "Do you know Lady Rockport?"

She nodded. "We're friends. It was her suggestion that I book a passage on this ship for Mr. Thornton."

"I know," he said.

She blinked. "But how—"

He hesitated, considering sharing his secret with her. Perhaps he would—later. Now he needed to learn about her. He waved his hand in a dismissive fashion his father had often demonstrated. "I have my sources."

Like being Lady Rockport's brother.

"You'll have people looking for you."

She sighed. "I left a note."

He had little faith that a few scribbles on paper would dissuade anyone from following the ship. Sisters of peers had family members with the resources to find them.

And I wanted to keep my identity secret.

He wanted to rail against her. He wanted to tell her just how much she'd surprised him. How much she'd allowed him to let his defenses down.

He considered his confused emotions. He'd liked her so much. He still did, despite everything. "You should have told me."

Guilt managed to flicker over her face, and her shoulders drooped downward.

"And I should have noticed," he murmured, though the words stuck in his throat.

He'd sworn before her. He'd given her drink and taken her out at night. He'd treated her like a friend. He'd completely abandoned every rule of etiquette and propriety. She hadn't bothered to mention she was in grave danger by boarding a ship filled with men, and she'd never told him that their long meetings were scandalous.

"People see what they expect. I doubt you could have anticipated that one of your passengers was a woman." She smiled. "And I do remember you being most suspicious at one point."

"I thought I imagined it. But when you placed my hand on your chest, I thought my desire for you was blinding me."

Her eyes widened at the word desire before her long lashes swooped down in a most adorable fashion.

"I was binding it," she said matter-of-factly, as if that could possibly be considered a normal statement.

He glanced at her still wet form and smirked. "But not now."

Her cheeks pinkened, and she drew her arms about her chest. "No. I didn't want the fabric to get wet and thought it so early that—"

"A ship never sleeps," he said.

"I see." He gestured to the bulging fall front on her breeches. "And that?"

"I sewed it." She smiled. "There had to be some good reason my governesses made me devote so much time to sewing. It's likely not completely anatomically correct..."

His lips twitched, and he forced them to sturdy and vowed to refrain from laughing.

She had to know that what she'd done had been completely, utterly inappropriate.

"I simply couldn't imagine that a woman would actually—"

"Disguise herself as a man to go to the West Indies?" Her voice was slightly bitter. "Interest herself in scientific pursuits? Do something besides marry her fiancé?"

She'd said many interesting words, but there was only one word he'd heard.

She has a fiancé.

How had he allowed himself to imagine she could be unattached? She was brave and intelligent, everything desirable.

The word hovered in the air, but she seemed oblivious to its significance.

"The poor man," he murmured.

"Because he has to marry me?" Hurt tore through her voice, and she inched away from him.

He blinked. "Because he's separated from you."

She drew in her breath, and her skin pinkened. Her hand moved to her throat, and he longed to help her. He longed to brush his fingers against the small hollow of her neck, and he longed to kiss it. He longed to suck the flesh, but instead he only gave her a wobbly smile.

He despised his sense of honor. Pirates certainly had a better idea. Not that he would ever, could ever, do anything to harm her.

He should be angry, but right now the only thing he wanted to do was pull her toward him. Whoever had placed the armchair so far from the sofa had been a madman.

He desired her. He craved her.

She'd stirred feelings in him even when he'd thought her a man, but now that her wet attire clung to her slender form, now that he could see the soft, feminine curves of her body...

He couldn't be in the same room as her pondering the faint vanilla scent that always emanated from her. He couldn't pull her toward him and undress her. He couldn't do all the things he longed to do with her.

He wanted to be inside her. His heartbeat thudded against his ribs, and blood pulsed through his body.

He shouldn't imagine it. He refused to picture himself guiding her onto his bed, even though his bed was tantalizingly close. He refused to imagine pulling that bathing costume from her body and resting her golden flesh against his white sheets. He refused to imagine taking her in his arms, and he certainly refused to imagine thrusting into her slick wetness.

He deserved to be given a medal for his current show of self-restraint.

She came from a good family. He considered her brother to be his very dearest friend. She was a debutante. And from the manner in which her eyes widened, she was an innocent.

Louisa bit her lower lip, and her gray eyes, the ones he'd once dismissed as colorless, swelled. Her long lashes flickered, and he ached to remove the doubt from her gaze. He ached to pull her toward him, but he had no right to desire such a thing. She would think he was simply taking advantage of her gender, doing all the things he'd warned her other, lesser men might attempt.

Wet breeches clung to her skin. She was the most scandalous thing he'd ever seen before. Salty water curled her hair, framing her face in a delicious manner. He wanted to trace the roll of drops with his tongue. He wanted to tear off her shirt. The opening parted in a manner that was not meant to be seductive but was the most enticing thing he'd ever seen.

"Louisa." His tongue seemed to thicken, less malleable in her presence. Never mind that none of his tutors in rhetoric had complained of his ability to communicate. Never mind that even the presence of pirates and Frenchmen on his ship hadn't hindered his ability to shout orders to his crew. Never mind that the clanging of swords slashing and the threat of cannonballs and coursing bullets hadn't halted his speech patterns.

Her skin was smooth and newly golden from the vast amounts of sunshine.

A woman like that wasn't supposed to sit primly on his sofa. A woman like that was supposed to lie splayed on his bed.

The flush that had been adorning her cheeks spread. He wanted to follow the color as it uncoiled over her body.

She stumbled to her feet. "I should undress. I—I need to change my attire."

Damnation.

She was shivering. He'd dragged her from the water and hadn't allowed her the opportunity to dry herself. The air might be warmer than in England, but that didn't mean a person should spend their time draped in damp attire.

"One moment." He grabbed a woolen blanket from his bedroom and pulled her to her feet, noting the manner in which her eyes widened.

The woman had turned into a temptress. And it didn't help that she'd begun to speak of undressing with an innocence that belonged to discussions of cutlery and flower arrangements.

He wanted to kiss her. It seemed a crime that his lips were not on her wide grin, that his hands were not wrapping around her waist. He wanted to crush her lithe body to his broader one. But he was the captain and she a passenger. She was under his protection, and kissing her was not something that would help her. Especially when he doubted he could stop at kissing her.

The vision of her form invaded his thoughts with the force of a warrior. Not that any warrior rivaled Louisa in charm. Her high, pert bosom seemed embedded in his mind, not shaken by however much he urged his mind to consider other issues. Her legs stretched endlessly, and her waist was tiny and more curved than he'd thought.

He longed to run his fingers over her skin, to memorize every curve with the thoroughness of an artist. He wanted to brush his lips against her body and taste her sun-kissed skin. Beads of water dripped from her hair to more interesting portions of her body. He'd never been so envious of the ocean. Her skin remained flushed, perhaps from the morning exercise, or perhaps from her current discomfort.

He was all too aware of how her breeches and shirt clung to her form in interesting manners. The woman's hair curled, and he longed to run his hands through the dark strands.

He gazed at her, still clutching the woolen blanket, and her eyes widened as if in fear. He cleared his throat and remembered to wrap the thick wool around her body. "This should warm you up."

"Thank you."

"Who is this...fiancé?" Rupert scowled. The act of forming the word fiancé seemed to rival the challenges of conducting warfare.

He did not want to speak about some other man with her. Whatever man it had been had been an absolute fool for ever letting her go. If he'd been that man, Rupert would never have surrendered her to some ship voyage.

"My mother desired me to find a husband. She is English you see, even though she's spent the past two decades in America. My father was American, but both my brothers went to English boarding schools and—"

"And your mother found you someone to marry." He turned and paced the room, as if the sound of his feet pounding against the wooden planks might distract him from his thoughts.

"Indeed."

He told himself it didn't matter if she married or not. He certainly couldn't offer himself as a substitute husband.

He had no intention of following his aristocratic peers into marriage, no matter how much it might please his parents. He'd long ago vowed never to have a wife worry about him when he was at sea.

"It doesn't matter." She giggled softly, though the sound managed to gnaw at him, and her eyes no longer sparkled. "I doubt we're engaged anymore."

"My condolences."

Louisa gave a sad smile. "I have likely broken my mother's heart by not leaping into his arms, grateful he might unburden me from my parents."

"But does the thought of not being with him break your heart?" He asked carefully.

"No," she murmured. "Not at all."

Oh.

"And why did you agree to marry him?"

She flushed. "I wasn't exactly considered prize material."

He shook his head. He despised the *ton.* He could just

imagine how they'd handled being around Louisa. He took her hands in his, trying to ignore the sharp surge of heat that threatened to career the once regular rhythm of his heart. He focused his gaze on her. "You are smart and brave and...beautiful. Never forget that."

The phrase didn't bring the smug smirk that normally came when he complimented women. She did not tilt her head and coyly compliment him, and she did not toss her hair and mock him for not coming to that realization sooner.

Instead she averted her gaze, and something in his heart ached.

"You mustn't exaggerate," she said.

"I mean it." He stroked his hand over her dark hair. Some of the strands were lighter, perhaps helped by the gleam of the sun and Louisa's practice of spending all day on deck.

They were so close.

He pulled her nearer to him, feeling her curves and her long legs against his own. Only inches separated her face from his, and even though all reason, all decency told him he should absolutely not narrow the gap between them, the thought that she could be inches away, when she should be right next to him seemed impossible.

*

Captain Rosse's head filled everything in her sight, and she realized a moment too late that he was going to kiss her.

Even though she'd never been kissed before.

Even though her hair was tousled in a distinctly unfeminine manner.

Even though she looked nothing like the elegant debutantes she'd been surrounded by all season.

Jewels did not sparkle from her neck, and perfectly curled locks did not frame her face. Her lips were never compared to rosebuds, and her eyes were never compared to the sky or a meadow. She wore no silk gown that gleamed under moonlight, helped by stones sewn into her bodice, and her freckled skin could never be compared to alabaster or porcelain. Her bosom did not curve in a majestic manner, and her hips were of a similarly ungenerous formation. Her locks could never be compared to gold, and were still somewhat damp, still salty.

Those facts did not dampen the heat in the captain's eyes.

He brushed warm fingers reverently over her face, and his breath lingered against her lips.

Her heart lurched, as if being tossed through a storm.

She didn't dare breathe, didn't dare even to blink, lest she discover him to be some mirage and his chiseled features shatter and move to the dream state to which they undoubtedly belonged.

Yet that delicious salty scent still pervaded the room, and the warmth of his hands seemed distinctly lifelike. Most unsuitable for a mirage.

His eyes darkened, and then—heavens—he swept her into his arms. Fire shot through her veins as she nestled against his firm muscles that bulged pleasingly from his shirt. He pulled her onto his lap, and then his lips were upon her. They captured hers with every bit the same force he must have used when battling the enemy.

His kiss deepened, strengthened, as if he were imbibing her.

The sparks coursing through her intensified, wilder, larger, more magnificent. She ran her hands over him, but no longer to ascertain his presence; there was nothing about the compilation of hard muscles and hot masculine skin that she could have conjured. Candlelight flickered over them, casting golden light from sconces and candelabras, utterly unaware of the magnificent form which they so casually illuminated.

The ship creaked, and she stilled, her heart lurching. They weren't alone. Some twenty-odd men were on the ship, and each one of them possessed the ability to ruin her further. She still wore masculine attire and her breeches-clad legs tangled with his.

A knock sounded on the door. "Cap'n?"

"Damnation." The captain—Rupert—stepped away from her. "It's time to set sail from Barbados."

She probably did remember how to speak, but right now all she could focus on was the memory of his lips on hers. Rupert's eyes softened, and he squeezed her hand again.

"I'll be right there." He called to Fergus and exited his quarters, leaving Louisa alone, as she realized everything, absolutely everything had changed.

Chapter
Eighteen

Mountains jutted from the coast, their sides angled downward with the straightness of the pyramids in her geography books. Palm trees fluttered in the breeze, and Louisa pushed her feet into the golden sand of St. Lucia.

Last night a storm had passed, and Conrad had brought some food to her cabin. She'd spent the night listening to the captain and his sailors shout above deck as rain pummeled, and waves jerked the ship into wild sways.

Today the sky had shifted from dark gray to a pleasing blue, and Louisa searched for a nearby cove. She hadn't abandoned her binding this time, and she'd chosen a sturdier shirt and breeches in which to swim.

Rupert flashed a smile at her as he strode from the water to where she lay stretched on the beach. Some sailors were about, and she strove to firm her expression as if she did not find it special at all that the captain's hair glinted in the sunlight, or that his torso was bare. His grin broadened, and he settled beside her.

She turned her head away as he neared, too conscious of his enticing scent of sea water and leather.

The sound was deep and warm, and she longed to bury her head against his chest.

She doubted that would count as being discreet, so instead she grasped hold of her diving helmet and pushed it over her head. Rupert's eyes widened, but then he laughed.

"I—I should go." Her legs were unsteady, and the helmet muffled her voice. At least the helmet managed to mask the warmth that soared over her cheeks. "Care to join?"

She hadn't thought the question overly forward, but Rupert's face paled, and he averted his gaze from her.

"I—I would rather not," he said.

"Oh."

Of course. They'd simply shared a kiss. And though the kiss had meant everything in the world to her, the man was experienced and had likely shared more kisses with women than he might count. Why should he desire to join her?

She focused on the crystal water. The place managed to exceed the beauty she'd envisioned. She should be content to focus on that, but her attention was distinctly focused on a certain sea captain.

She quickened her pace. The turquoise waves lapped around her feet, and seashells sparkled from the shore.

The captain reclined on the sand. He'd stripped his shirt off, and sweat gleamed from his bare torso. She wished he might join her. His distaste for the water seemed at odds with his profession, though perhaps he was not the only seaman to have a mistrust of the ocean. After all, the man spent so long working on keeping his ship upright in the waves that it must seem unnatural to submerge into the very waters he worked so hard to prevent his ship from toppling into.

She lengthened her strides, even as the water made the fact more difficult, and finally dove into the ocean.

Myriad vibrant colors confronted her. Jeweled fish flitted over coral. This was a world, as clear and as distinct as the one she'd just stepped from. Schools of fish swam together, moving matter-of-factly. Louisa wasn't certain what they could see, these tiny creatures, but she could wonder at this distinct world. The blue sky seemed an unequal partner to the ocean below. Even the birds that flapped their colorful wings, the parrots that squawked from branches, even they could not rival the wonders in the ocean.

She wanted to immerse herself in the warm waters forever and exit only to rejoin the captain.

*

The chit lacked any idea of how beautiful she was. He didn't want any of the sailors to find out there was a woman on board. They showed no hesitation in bedding the least attractive harlots, and he didn't want to think about the strength of their vigor were they to bed a woman of actual beauty.

For whatever he'd thought of Louisa before, and he'd despised the uncharitable thoughts toward her, largely ascribed to her hideously colored oversized dress, he could not deny her beauty.

Temptation herself was on this ship.

He kept watch over her as she sank deeper into the water.

I should join her.

She hadn't understood why he hadn't wanted to accompany her, and he wrapped his arms around his chest and focused on the familiar landscape. The aqua water lapped up the white sandy shore, and bright-colored birds waddled near the waves or perched on the branches of tropical trees.

Perhaps if he stared at the sapphire expanse before him, he might forget the pool of pink in the ocean, and he might forget calling Jasper's name to no avail. Perhaps he might forget the frantic search through the ever-expanding pool of pink until he pulled his best friend's bullet-riddled body from the waves.

He gritted his teeth and continued to keep watch as Louisa explored depths he never might.

Chapter
Nineteen

The captain had stayed on the shore the entire day,
working under the palm trees.

Louisa returned to him and took off her diving helmet.
She knew her hair must look horrid, but the smile he
gave her seemed almost tender.

"Let's return to the ship," he said.

She nodded and followed him over the sand. Heat
swirled through her body, as they walked to *The Sapphire
Princess*. The sailors greeted them, and Rupert announced
they could find him in his quarters.

The mood shifted inexplicably, as if her body had only
now recognized the humidity. The air seemed heavy, and
the space between them seemed impossibly long.

She stopped at her door, but his hungry gaze swooped
over her. "Join me. We have a discussion to continue."

He opened the door to his quarters, and she felt as
if she were standing on a precipice, and everything that

was sensible urged her to retreat to her windowless cabin adorned only with research materials.

Her breath seemed trapped inside her chest, caught by the sudden-ratcheting of her heart. "Very well."

She entered his quarters, and he closed the door behind them.

His blue eyes rested on her with all the force of the ocean on a windy day. His jaw was set, and his knuckles tightened over the sides of his chair. He removed his coat, and the buttons glittered in the candlelight. Shadows danced beneath the warm rays of the candles as the ship rocked gently in the water, and she inhaled the faint smell of salt.

She swallowed hard. "Wh-what did you desire to speak about?"

His smile broadened, and his gaze would not have looked out of place on a tiger.

"I believe I was telling you how beautiful you are."

He neared her, and she was conscious of the dark hair that curled from his chest; the men she was accustomed to covered their necks in intricately tied cravats. "I found you distinctly more appealing than any of those ladies at that...establishment."

"Oh," she breathed.

"Even when I thought you were a man, I still found you appealing. Even though the fact was most confusing."

"And now—"

"I still find you appealing." He chuckled. "Extraordinarily so."

The statement should have made her smile, but her body seemed to be far more preoccupied in noting the fact that he was striding toward her.

"You have no idea the self-restraint I'm drawing upon

to not take you into my arms, to not ravish you utterly and completely."

"Oh." The word came out as a throaty moan. "Truly?"

"Truly." He nodded, and her heart squeezed again. She'd never been so conscious of it in her life.

"Perhaps that would not be so dreadful."

His eyes widened, and she swallowed hard. She'd sounded just like a brazen harlot.

"My dear Louisa," Rupert said, and his eyes sparkled. "You may be an innocent, but you are entirely correct. It must be all that scientific training you do. If you find yourself shy when I compliment your appearance, I have another solution for how we might continue where we were last interrupted."

"Oh?"

"Kissing you. We could continue kissing."

Even though she still wore breeches, even though *he* still wore breeches, pleasure sluiced through her body. She wrapped her arms about the rippling muscles of his back, the outline hardly hidden by the thin shirt, and grasped hold as if she were at risk of floating away.

And then she really was floating, and she realized he was carrying her to his bed.

The mattresses sank under their weight, aided by the loose rope mesh, and he lay closer to her than propriety would allow.

His chest crushed against her bosom and something hard and long and very, very masculine, settled against her stomach.

Rupert's eyes gleamed, the force greater than that of the sunshine cascading off the waves earlier, and he directed his hardness, so it pressed against her most intimate place.

"Please," she gasped, adjusting her body, so that delicious, sinful pleasure would more thoroughly press against her center.

Her breath became more unsteady, mingling with his equally uneven pant.

*

The woman was clad in breeches and a shirt. Her long legs stretched to unspeakable lengths. Her still damp white stockings emphasized the slenderness of her ankles, and he longed to trace the soft curve of those ankles to the more distinct curve of her hips. The buttons on her fall front highlighted the unusualness of her attire, but he knew what he would find if he were to unbutton those two buttons below her waist would be all wonderful.

A pretty pink ascended her cheeks, dancing with her freckles, and he gazed back at her. He would be content to gaze at her for a long time.

He tilted his head, and the pink color darkened. She thrust her lashes downward, and she fiddled her delicate fingers.

Rupert moved his hand over Louisa's shirt. The sleeves puffed in a similar manner to his own, and he longed to see her form. He untied Louisa's cravat, finding the perspective odd as he grasped hold of the crisp linen as he would his own.

The mirror image ended there, for the neck that was exposed was most certainly not of the masculine variety. Her long white throat gleamed in the candlelight, unmarred by anything so masculine as an Adam's apple, and he lowered his lips to the bare flesh and sucked.

He clasped her more tightly in his arms, as if the tiniest

of distances between them was unseemly. He despised the cut of the shirt. At least women's dresses were easily lowered. The tailor for this shirt had clearly not sought to give this item of apparel similar advantages.

"Up," he gasped and pulled her toward him and removed her shirt.

Fabric still bound her chest, and he cursed the swath of linen. He'd never despised the material so much in his life. His fingers trembled as he unfastened the tightly wound cloth.

If he'd had any lingering doubts of her femininity before this, they'd certainly vanished when he set aside the last of the linen.

Her bosom arched before him. Though he'd seen the curve through her damp shirt when she'd swum, that was nothing to the sight before him now.

He captured them in his hands, caressing them. He rounded her beautifully-formed bosom with his fingers, circling the warm flesh. Her rose-red peaks pebbled and firmed beneath his fingers, and he dipped his head down to one of the pink areolas and captured it with his mouth, while his hand continued to tease and encircle the other one.

"Rupert," Louisa moaned, and the sound of his name on her tongue caused his excitement to grow.

Her fingers pulled him closer to her, playing with the short strands of his hair, and he moved his mouth over her, enjoying the manner in which she writhed beside him, enjoying as her breath grew increasingly uneven and frantic as he sought to memorize every part of her body with his tongue and fingers.

"Please," she moaned, her voice rough.

Desire coursed through his body, moving with the sort

of rapidity he more associated with ships fleeing pirates. He moved his fingers below the waist of her breeches, cursing that Louisa had evidently stolen a garment not devoid of fashion, for its opening stretched to her waist. He scrambled up and flipped her over, so he might unfasten the flaps at her back that tightened about her waist.

"Tell me if you would like me to stop," he said. "I can stop."

She shook her head adamantly. "No. Never."

Never.

The word echoed in his mind, and he removed her socks and glided her breeches downward. Her long legs splayed before him.

He skimmed his hands over her legs. They felt silky beneath his touch. They were perfectly formed, stronger than that of most women of high society who maintained their figures by depriving themselves of food, strolling through ballrooms, their pace always hampered by the throng of the *ton* surrounding them, and more occasionally by managing to not topple from their horses as they ambled through Hyde Park.

No, he'd never been with a woman like Louisa. Of that, he was absolutely certain.

"My darling." He smiled. Most higher society women bedded with their clothes on. Louisa's unconventional outfit had necessitated an unconventional approach to lovemaking.

Her cheeks flushed, perhaps at the term of endearment, and pride pulsed through him. He slid his shirt off.

In the next moment her hands were upon him, running her fingers over every muscle.

*

Louisa brushed her lips against his chest, capturing his tawny peaks as he'd done for her. The man moaned beneath her, causing her lips to turn up.

Perhaps if she concentrated on kissing him, she might pretend she would always remember the salty taste of his skin and that she'd always remember what it felt like to be clasped in his arms. Perhaps she could pretend he would never leave her in Falmouth with her brother Arthur, and they might be together for longer. *Much, much longer.* Rupert removed his breeches and flung them on the desk. They contrasted with the neatly organized papers and books already there, and she smiled.

And then he was upon her, claiming her with his lips.

She realized she hadn't understood the true force of positive adjectives. Wonderful and superb took on new, greater meanings.

His fingers continued to brush over her as he continued to mark her body, dwelling on areas that she'd found utterly uninteresting. He kissed the arch of her neck, moving toward her ear. He pulled her earlobe into the mouth, and every nerve in her being seemed to sing.

His every move was skilled, perfect.

"Please." She didn't know what she was begging for. He lowered his mouth and trailed kisses over her stomach to the tender skin on her inner thighs. His long fingers swept over the juncture of the pulsating core between her hips, and she gasped.

His fingers stroked her center and sent blood tingling. Her body throbbed around his assertive fingers, and she eagerly sought his mouth with hers.

Firm muscles pressed against her soft curves and drove her deeper into the bed. Her heart lurched into a new rhythm, dictated by the dance his fingers made.

"You're so moist. So warm," he said, awe in his voice.

He stroked her hair tenderly. "Some women say this portion can be painful."

"Then so be it."

"Fortunately," he mused, and his lips spread into a cocky grin, "You are in excellent hands."

He tilted her hips, and she felt him push into her.

He was large.

He was firm.

And he was inside her.

She inhaled, and he paused, stroking her hair as she adjusted to the sensation of a throbbing, pulsating member inside her. Of *Rupert* inside her. She'd cast aside her maidenhood, her last shred of respectability, but only wonder soared through her.

He pulled her into his sturdy embrace, and she clutched hold of his now slick shoulders. A sheen of sweat glimmered over his torso, managing to make him appear even more Adonis-like.

He began to rock inside her, and then his thrusts grew stronger, more forceful. "You're so lovely. And so...tight."

She smiled at him, uncertain what was causing his eyes to soften, but happy that the moment seemed to bring him pleasure.

Something rippled inside her, some need awakened by his rhythmic thrusts, and she pushed her hips forward, meeting him. The fire spread, and Rupert's pace quickened.

More frantic. More fast. More...fantastic.

The frenzy heightened, and energy surged through

her, washing through every nerve of her being. She breathed in, and then, as he continued to thrust inside her, continued to brush against her very core, she gasped.

Pleasure cascaded through her, and she clung to his neck. He continued to push into her, in an ever more frenzied rhythm. He spread kisses over her face. "My dearest."

She glided from her crest of bliss. Satisfaction surged through her, mingled with a sudden tiredness.

His gaze seemed to grow more tender, and his pace slowed. His lips once again found hers, and their tongues seemed to speak in a way that they could not, caressing each other.

She moved her hands over his body, enjoying the textures as they traveled from his short hair to the stubble of his cheeks, to his multitude of muscles.

He wrapped his arms more tightly around her back, pulling himself deeper into her body, as if that's where he belonged.

"You're so warm, so tight, so...amazing."

"I'm yours," she said, and the words seemed to jolt him. He thrust inside her, growing more forceful. He pushed himself in and out, desperation evident. He groaned and growled, as if some animal possessed him, as if he'd let her see his inner beast.

He finally moaned and pulled himself from her core. Hot seed soared from his length, spilling over her belly and breasts and he collapsed on top of her, once again kissing her.

"My dearest," he moaned, pulling her tightly toward him, as if he couldn't fathom the thought of taking the time to clean now; now when he might be holding her in his arms.

She smiled at the happiness in his gaze, and her heart leaped as he continued to crush her toward him, as his eyelids flickered downward. Even in sleep he did not seem to desire to be parted from her. She gave into the blissful sensation and relaxed in his sturdy, encompassing embrace.

Chapter Twenty

A knock sounded on the door, and Rupert reluctantly slid from her.

"One moment," his voice boomed easily and authoritatively, but then he kissed her lips and gave her a boyish grin.

He smoothed his tousled hair and tightened his cravat so that he looked like he'd been doing nothing improper.

He shut the door, and she lounged over the sheets. She'd never felt more wanton.

Voices sounded outside, and she pulled the sheet over her.

Closing her eyes only brought up images: Images of bare skin and firm muscles, of sweat dripping from sun-kissed skin, of all things absolutely forbidden, all things unthinkable for nice younger sisters of dukes.

"We're gonna go back to the girls, captain. Wanna come with us?"

"I have decided to stay on board," Rupert said more stiffly.

"But we've hardly seen you! And who knows when we'll next see so many ladies!"

Louisa's heart tumbled downward.

"Not this time," Rupert said.

Louisa sat up.

Soon she would be gone, and he would be free to visit the most deprived sections of the West Indies. She was something for his amusement, something of greater closeness and practicality than the whores on the island.

She pulled on her shirt and slid back into her breeches.

She was behaving foolishly. This was her one escape, her one adventure, and she should be grateful that Rupert desired to spend their last days together with her. But despite all her logic, her chest still managed to clench.

Perhaps hearts were never known for being logical.

She moved from the bed and sat down at the desk all the same. She needed to give herself some semblance of propriety. Rupert continued to speak with the sailor, laughing with him about various past misadventures.

She settled onto the chair and flickered her eyes to the desk. A red-sealed letter was splayed open.

She didn't mean to read the name, but the address was so unexpected that it seemed to immediately sear into her mind.

Rupert had told her to call him by his given name, and before that she'd referred to him as "Captain," but he'd never once told her to call him "My Lord." None of his many sailors referred to him like that.

And yet, here on the paper, the curved words were clear. He was a lord. And even more than that—he was an earl.

Goodness.

He was Lady Rockport's brother! Cordelia had spoken of him.

He must have thought her so foolish. Confessing that no man in the *ton* desired her, despite her connections. The man's father was a duke.

Her chest tightened. She'd stopped being aware of the rock of the ship, but now she felt every wave as it pummeled the hull. The ship seemed to lurch uneasily, and she buttoned her clothes.

He'd given her grief for not sharing her secret with him—but even after she'd revealed that she was a woman in disguise. Even when she'd made herself incredibly vulnerable by confessing that she was a woman—of the young, unmarried sort, hundreds of miles removed from any chaperone—he hadn't shared his secret.

And why should he? He was an earl, he would become a duke, and she was merely a silly girl who couldn't land a dance partner, much less a paragon of masculinity like him.

The murmurings slowed, and she became aware of Rupert's footsteps approaching. She swallowed hard.

She should return to the bed and feign ignorance of the letter. She should just accept their remaining days for what they were.

But instead her stomach tightened, and she felt that if she were to stand, she would struggle to do so for long, like the female travelers she'd seen on her journey across the Atlantic from England.

She clutched the letter in her hand and smoothed the corners. She stared at the words, but the letters did not shift, she hadn't misread, and in the next moment the door swung open.

"Loui—" Rupert's voice halted. He'd noticed the letter.

Louisa's lips firmed, and she set the note down.

"Yes, my lord?" She attempted levity, but sarcasm rippled through her voice despite her best intentions.

"I should have put that away," he said. "How idiotic of me."

He'd chided her for her deception, but he'd never bothered to tell her his true name. Or at least not his true last name, and she'd been more intimate with him than anyone.

She despised the hesitation over his face and sighed. "Obviously I won't share your title with the others on board."

"Or off board." His speech was careful as if he were handling her with the attention he might give an unruly puppy amongst his best boots.

"Naturally." She pulled her arms over her chest. "So Captain Rosse is just a name you invented?"

He sighed. "I am a captain."

*

She knows.

All his instincts told him to leave it at that. She was nodding. She would accept that. But this was *Louisa*. And even though he'd vowed to tell no one his real name—though his family had managed to track them down, using their vast wealth to fulfill their curiosity—he found that he actually desired to tell her.

"Jasper Rosse was my best friend," Rupert said. "His parents were servants on one of my father's estates. I grew up playing with him in the field and creek nearby." He smiled. "We used to play sailors—row a little boat up the creek and sing sailors' tunes."

Louisa settled back in the chair. He didn't deserve the understanding look she gave him.

"Jasper always wanted to be a captain. When the war happened. Well, it was simple. We joined the navy." He smiled. "My sister always thought the ships impressive anyway."

"He *was* your best friend?"

"Yes. Not that I have one now." He hesitated. The statement felt wrong in his mouth, and he realized he did have a best friend—Louisa. How had that happened? Women weren't supposed to hold that position. He shook his head. The point of the conversation was not to mull over Louisa's importance to him. "Jasper always wanted to be a captain. And he would have been—I'm sure of it. He was good. Really good. Completely fearless. He would climb the riggings in the middle of a storm when other sailors would be paralyzed with fear. He was smart, and everyone respected him. But then—"

"He died?" Louisa asked softly.

He nodded, and his heart twisted as it always did when he considered it.

"It was war. An American ship attacked. Our ship was destroyed, and we had to jump off."

"And then?"

"A cannon must have struck him. One moment he was beside me, and the next, the water was filled with blood and his body." He glanced away.

"I'm so sorry, Rupert."

He shrugged. "I got to live."

"And you took his name?"

"To honor him. He never got a chance to be a captain, but I wanted to make sure he got the chance to be one." He buried his head in his hands. "It sounds foolish."

"It sounds like you were a good friend." She frowned. "Is that why you don't swim?"

He nodded. "I know how to of course. And I still find it pretty. But the thought of being in the salty water, in the waves—I can't do it."

She took his hand in hers, and her warm fingers rubbed against his palm. The gesture soothed him.

"I shouldn't complain," he said. "I'm lucky to be alive."

"I'm very happy you're alive," she said. "But I know how hard it is to pretend. It must have been so difficult."

Her fingers continued to play a gentle rhythm over his hands, but he took her into his arms and melted into her as they kissed.

*

She was certainly no longer an innocent.

They'd repeated their lovemaking. Over and over again.

She'd taken to researching during the day, capturing fish in buckets and recording them when the ship sailed toward Falmouth, and diving into the ocean when the ship was anchored. Weeks passed.

But at night, she went to his room, grateful the sailors on the ship knocked on her door with less frequency than the chambermaids in her manor homes.

And it was always wonderful.

She tilted her head at Rupert.

Candlelight flickered over the hard planes of his body, casting him in a golden glow. She stroked the lines of his muscles, comfortable in brushing her fingers over areas that should be wholly unnatural for her. "I am enjoying this adventure."

"I wish you could stay." He laughed. "At some point I would be bound to give myself away. I can only show so much fascination for fish before Fergus grows even more suspicious."

"Fergus finds you lacking in intellect?" She raised her eyebrows, and he responded by slapping her with a pillow and then pulling her into his arms.

The next moments involved rather more kissing, and her heart was occupied with the feel of his against her.

"I wish it could be true." He brushed his hands over her hair, and his eyes flared as he continued to explore her body with his hands as if he sought to memorize every curve. "I wish you could stay with me forever."

"And why would it not be possible? If I stayed as...me?" Her heart pattered more uncomfortably now, as if conscious her question might be perceived as unfeminine.

"You're serious?" He halted his exploration of her body, and she didn't realize how much she could crave the sensation of his fingers. "My sweet darling. That would be amazing."

Her heart beat faster, but then his face clouded. "Unfortunately I would not confine you to the fate of some sea captains, forced to gaze out their windows in hopes of seeing their husbands' ships."

"And what if I continued to sail with you?"

"You mean as Mr. Thornton?"

"No."

Realization flickered over his face. "I would love to have you by my side. But it's impossible. The West Indies is no place for a woman. This ship is no place for a woman."

"But I enjoy it—"

"Nelson called this region Hell. There are many, many risks involved in traveling here."

"That was his opinion."

"People respect his opinion greatly."

Louisa tried to give a nonchalant sigh. She suspected this conversation had nothing to do with Nelson at all. He didn't want her. It was that simple.

"Look." He inhaled. "There are all sorts of diseases here. Malaria and such. In the Royal Navy nobody wanted to be assigned here. Few people even wanted to join the navy at all—that's how people like Fergus were practically kidnapped by the government in order to work on the boats."

"And yet, here you are," she said, her voice bitter. "And your men seem content."

He shrugged. "A coincidence. Besides you would get bored here. No wives last long on ships. Not that many attempt a life beside their husbands. You wouldn't be able to decorate, you wouldn't be able to have your cook make you the latest dishes. There are sailors always around. It's a dreadful life. That's for certain."

She smiled tightly. "It was just a musing. Just a silly daydream. I wasn't the least bit serious."

"Oh."

"I—I wasn't referring to staying with specifically you."

He frowned, and her cheeks burned. Naturally he hadn't been taken in by her lie. Naturally he saw her as just another female, taken by his charm. He'd likely had this conversation with other women, women more suited to tie themselves to him. Women who didn't dress as men, who didn't marvel at marine life with the enthusiasm they should be giving their own appearance.

She laughed weakly. She was glad—so glad he enjoyed

her company, but she wondered whether it was possible that he just thought her a plaything. She didn't want to be just a woman he'd been clever enough to discover on board.

She wanted it to be *more*. But wasn't that thought naïve? Louisa prided herself on her lack of naivety, but could there be anything more foolish than imagining that Rupert could be anything more than momentarily intrigued by her? It was probably more a testament to his virility than her attractiveness that he even deigned to spend time with her now.

She'd met other men, and all of them had been happy to abandon her when it became clear that another woman was available for them to speak to. Dancing with her had been a chore they'd seemed to hate, as if the fact they were forced to chitchat with her was proof of an inability to charm anyone else.

She waited for his shoulders to relax, but they didn't.

"I suppose I should go back to my cabin," she suggested.

"Nonsense." He blew out the candle and pulled her toward him. "I would not have you make me so distressed."

She nodded and leaned into his arms, unsure of everything as he tightened his grasp around her.

*

Something seemed to have changed.

She'd stopped teasing him with her hands, and her body had grown more rigid.

He pulled her closer to him, ran his fingers through her

hair as if that gesture alone might bring back some of that earlier ease.

He tried to ignore her words.

She hadn't truly meant a marriage.

He was sure of it.

Because she was the most intelligent person he knew. She came from a good family, and she had better things waiting for her, whatever she might think now.

He'd abandoned his family too hastily. He wanted her to think more before she did the same. And he couldn't bear to ask her to stay with him, knowing the risk that she'd place herself in to do it. His best friend had been with him in the West Indies, and he had died, right before him. Rupert hadn't been able to protect Jasper—how was he supposed to protect Louisa?

No, it was better to pretend that she'd never said it.

Better to enjoy the moment now and not worry about the future.

Chapter
Twenty-one

The wide expanse of sky and ocean no longer comforted Rupert. Knowledge that the world was grander and more beautiful than anything he'd once imagined in Hampshire did not halt his musings that he should do everything possible to keep Louisa by his side. *Forever.*

The ocean might resemble liquid sapphire, the foam that crested over the waves might sparkle with a vigor typically found in diamonds, but none of that meant anything without Louisa. They were approaching Falmouth, and soon they would see the familiar pastel buildings.

His heart clenched, and even Louisa seemed to favor standing beside him than doing her beloved research, even though this would be an optimal day to conduct it.

"Ahoy! There's a ship yonder." A sailor shouted from the top of the mast, and Rupert and Conrad turned to gaze at a vessel in the distance.

"Reckon that might be a pirate ship." Suspicion filled Conrad's voice, and Rupert gazed through his telescope at the fast-moving boat. It was distinctly odd that the ship was heading directly toward them.

"Pirates?" Louisa's voice wobbled.

Rupert sighed. Pirates were just the sort of reason why he and Louisa should not be together. "Life is dangerous on sea."

There wasn't anything romantic about it. Why couldn't the woman see that? Most sensible people stayed away from the West Indies. Even the adventurers preferred to while away their time in the Alps or the Pyrenees, too aware of the ease of contracting malaria here. Death came in many forms in the Caribbean.

No, he couldn't let Louisa be any part of that.

He stared at the vessel. "There are all sorts of pirates in the Caribbean."

"A lot of them are British," Louisa said. "And I believe you call them privateers."

"Did you tell Mr. Thornton about our past?" Conrad asked.

"I do know some things," Louisa insisted. She grabbed the telescope and peered at the boat. "So what's the protocol? Do we all get pistols now?"

"We need to ascertain who they are first." He forced his gaze away. It wouldn't do if she saw his lips twitch.

"Naturally," Louisa said. "I rather thought you would possess the expertise for that. Now—are we looking for a particular flag? They can't all have a skull and crossbones on them."

"They don't." This time Rupert couldn't keep his smile from spreading. He coughed. "But they can be dangerous all the same. You should go below deck."

"And leave you without another pair of hands on deck?" She frowned. "I've been to England. If I can shoot foxes and pheasants, I bloody well can shoot pirates. It will bring me much more pleasure."

Conrad and Fergus looked startled. They hadn't had the pleasure of spending as much time with Louisa as Rupert had.

"They must make the men in Massachusetts very brave. No wonder they started the Revolutionary War," Fergus said.

"Don't forget we also won the war," Louisa said.

"I don't think any Englishman can forget," Fergus said miserably.

"And then we started the War of 1812," Louisa said. "And we beat you again. Even though we had to build our navy from scratch."

"That might be a slight exaggeration," Rupert insisted and took the telescope from Louisa's hands. "You did lose Canada."

"Fiddle-faddle," Louisa declared. "We never had Canada. We can't be sorry we don't have it now."

"If we could only get some vicious men like you in Cornwall," Fergus said, viewing Louisa in wonder.

Rupert smiled, but his gaze remained fixed on the speeding vessel directed straight at them.

Jamaica was in sight, a destination filled with sugar, sandy beaches, a ground that did not sway and rock, and imposing mountains.

But the vessel was headed for *The Sapphire Princess.*

He scowled. He'd like to see the vessel try to attack them. It wouldn't be the first time pirates had dared to target his crew.

Not that he was going to detail his past experiences

with Louisa now. He might not possess much sanity when it came to her, but by God, he would hang onto the faint modicum of it he still possessed.

"Fergus, take Mr. Thornton downstairs," he ordered.

"But—" Louisa's voice was more high-pitched than she tended to use when wearing breeches, and her face flushed, and she coughed.

"Now!" He growled at Fergus, and the sailor returned a solemn nod before he yanked hold of Louisa's arm.

"The captain prides himself on taking care of his passengers," Fergus said. "If 'e 'ad wanted his passengers to fight pirates, 'e wouldn't 'ave asked for a fare."

Rupert's shoulders relaxed somewhat as Louisa's footsteps became fainter, but he retained his focus on the strange ship.

His crew could take any attackers; he was certain.

Still... This served as a good reminder that he needed to protect Louisa, and that he couldn't give in to the insurmountable temptation to have her by his side forever.

His chest squeezed.

Blast. Why did he feel like he was making a mistake even with pirates in obvious proximity?

He withdrew his pistol and confirmed with the gunmen that the cannons were ready to be fired.

But as the ship approached, he only saw the flag of the bloody former colonials. He frowned. Was the United States preparing to start a third war against Britain? He wouldn't put such an action past the blasted upstarts, though it would be bloody bad luck if the ex-colonials began with his ship. *The Sapphire Princess* might be grand, but it wasn't exactly *The Chesapeake.*

The vessel cut through the water, sending streams of sparkling sapphire soaring through the air, and the people on deck scowled at him with a ferociousness that even managed to exceed his experience with pirates.

"Hey! Hey, you!" A man with a strong American accent waved at them. "You better stop!"

"We command you halt!" A middle-aged man in tight breeches thundered, his hair similarly tousled, his gaze similarly irate, though his voice was distinctly British.

It was the sort of upper-class accent, honed from school at Eton or Harrow, that Rupert immediately recognized.

Because at one point he'd had the same accent.

These men were not friendly, and he thanked heavens again that Louisa was below deck.

"You've taken my son's new bride," the British man shouted.

Rupert scowled, even as his stomach toppled downward, even though he wasn't prone to suffering from sea sickness. He glared at the pompously attired men. They were fools if they thought he would ever give Louisa up, no matter how much they shouted, and how close their vessel came to his own.

"We ain't got no woman here!" Fergus leaned over the ledge and hollered. He turned to Rupert. "Those men must be mad."

Rupert tightened his lips.

"Nonsense," the Englishman bellowed. "The ship's name is painted in bright colors. Who is the captain?"

"I am the ship's captain," Rupert thundered. "Captain Rosse."

Rupert frowned at the familiar lie, but if he was going to start telling the truth, he bloody well wasn't going to start with this abominable man.

"Not that *The Sapphire Princess* has anything to do with women," Fergus volunteered.

"Don't worry, lad," the man said. "You're a plebeian; you wouldn't understand. I am Sir Seymour Amberly. You may have heard of me. I am a baronet from the great county of Yorkshire!"

Fergus blinked. "Reckon I've heard of Yorkshire... Ain't that way up north?"

Sir Seymour beamed, evidently undeterred by the bright sunbeams, and squinted toward them. "Finest part of England it is! No wonder you're sailing in this part of the world. You don't know what you're missing in Yorkshire."

Sir Seymour turned away from them, and Rupert noticed two nicely attired men in the shadows. Their faces were obscured.

"Cecil! Cecil my boy," Sir Seymour said. "It's going to be fine. Papa's found the man who's stolen your bride."

So this was Louisa's fiancé. Louisa had supposed the engagement would be over, but instead her fiancé cared so much for he was chasing her across the ocean.

He stared at the man who'd planned to marry Louisa. He wanted to despise the man, though he was a paler, weaker version of his father. He wore a ruffled frock coat, a deep aubergine color that explained some of the sweat dampening the man's face since actual passion or anger did not seem to be displayed.

His starched cravat failed to mask the man's weak chin. He looked burned by the sun, and Rupert was once again grateful his own complexion did not tend to suffer from that particular affliction.

"I'm telling you, we ain't got no woman here," Fergus shouted again.

"Liar!" Sir Seymour voice barreled through the air. "My son's fiancée is on this ship! We've tracked you down! The marriage will take place."

The baronet removed a musket, as if he intended to shoot Rupert right there and then.

Rupert smirked and raised his pistol and directed it calmly at Sir Seymour. The baronet was mad if he thought he'd ever manage to defeat *The Sapphire Princess*, no matter if he came from Yorkshire.

Muskets were not lauded for an ability to fire at long range, and he was certain their range would not be improved when held on a swaying ship. He glanced at his sailors. "Think you remember how to attack a ship, lads?"

"Aye, aye, Cap'n!" the men shouted with glee, and he smiled. They were a bloody good crew.

"Direct the cannons at the ship," he called out, his voice roared over the wind.

Sir Seymour's face whitened, and he tossed the musket to his son.

"Father!" The man's pale flesh had pinkened under the bright sun, and he slicked back his damp hair. His discomfited demeanor was not lessened by his foppish attire.

"That would be a very bad idea," Rupert announced. "One shot and these cannons will blow your vessel to bits." He scowled. "*Small* bits."

"And 'e's good at ducking," Fergus announced proudly.

Rupert grinned. "I'm good at lots of things." He turned to his crew. "*Now.*"

The sailors chuckled and shouted curses with glee. They hauled rope onto the mast, tying it tightly, and then one by one they grabbed hold of the rope, ran, and then sailed through the air until they dropped onto the other ship. They withdrew knives from their belts, a weaker substitute to their former swords, but weapons which still managed to make the faces on the other ship whiten.

"Now line up," Conrad ordered the crew of the other ship. "I don't like surprises."

"Neither do I," Fergus roared, and his red hair glinted under the harsh Caribbean light.

The men's knees on the other ship seemed to quiver, and he assessed Louisa's fiancé, the man who had more claim to her than he did. The man squinted at him, though he did not direct the pistol toward him. Rupert smirked. Clearly Sir Seymour's progeny had reached higher heights of virtue than his sire, for he removed the ammunition from the musket and lowered the barrel.

"Quite intelligent," Rupert said coolly. "Now. Once my men return I want you to turn your boat around and go as far away from us and as quickly away from us as you can."

"You don't want to steal anything?" Fergus eyed Sir Seymour's velvet outfit. "Reckon men like that might have some fancy things."

"Sir!" The American man looked outraged.

"Cecil!" Sir Seymour ordered. "Tell the man about how your heart is broken! How you'll fight the man to the death! How—"

"You want to fight me to the death?" Rupert raised his eyebrows and rolled up his sleeves.

Mr. Amberly's face merely whitened.

"No," Rupert said, glancing again at Mr. Amberly. He'd already taken something quite valuable from the man. "We'll let them go."

Fergus sighed. "It's no fun being decent. I'll tell the other sailors. They'll be mighty disappointed."

Rupert shrugged.

"The man needs to return something," a male voice declared.

Rupert paused. He knew that voice.

Arthur Carmichael stepped out from behind a mast. "I always did want to see you capture a ship. Congratulations, it's every bit as impressive as the reports."

Normally Rupert might have smiled, but there was something about the gleam in the man's eyes that did not appeal to him. "What are you doing here, Carmichael?"

"I think you know," his longtime friend said.

"Should I shoot 'im?" Fergus asked.

Rupert sighed. "Hold your fire. All of you."

His men let out a disappointed wail, but they obeyed. He'd trained them well.

He made his way onto the other ship until he faced Arthur Carmichael.

The man glowered at him. "Where's my sister?"

"She doesn't want to see anyone."

"She's nineteen," Carmichael said. "She doesn't know what she wants."

"She's happy," Rupert insisted. "*We're* happy."

"Truly?" Carmichael sounded startled, and his eyes softened.

For a moment.

He soon frowned. "You can't take her. You know what life here is like." He gestured to Mr. Amberly. "This man wants to marry her. He can offer a good, safe life in considerable comfort."

Rupert's heart squeezed, but he lowered his voice. "Did you tell them about me?"

"I vowed never to betray your trust."

"I wouldn't want them to find out I'm an earl."

"Damnation." Carmichael sighed and gentled his voice. "Did nobody tell you?"

Rupert frowned.

"You must have left just before the news," Carmichael mused. "I suppose it's up to me. Your father's dead. So technically you're a duke, and I would advise you to go back to England to claim your estate.

Father is dead?

He hadn't seen him one last time. His father had asked to see him, and he'd refused, not wanting to delay his journey. Lord knew he'd only given himself a short sojourn in Brighton, just so he wouldn't succumb to any temptation to make the journey to Hampshire, so that he wouldn't feel foolish if his visit with his sister was uncomfortable or a trap.

I've been a fool.

"This doesn't change anything," Carmichael said. "Just because you're a duke, it doesn't mean you're fit to marry my sister. You're too wild, too unpredictable. I can't have you break her heart." Carmichael glanced at Cecil Amberly. "Whatever that man's faults are, he won't break her heart."

The man was right. Rupert's life was too dangerous.

Jasper died.

It might be beautiful here, but it was dangerous.

Carmichael fixed a steely stare at him.

Rupert wanted to resist. He could resist. He'd already taken their vessel. It would be easy to sail on, keeping

Louisa at his side, right where she said she wanted to be, right where *he* wanted her to be.

Happiness was so close.

He swallowed hard. Carmichael was right. He couldn't subject Louisa to such a life, no matter how much he would miss her. His heart ached, but he turned to Fergus. "Please bring Mr. Thornton."

Chapter
Twenty-two

A knock sounded on the door.

"Mr. Thornton. You're wanted above deck."

Louisa widened her eyes. They wanted her to fight after all. She swung her door open.

This was about protecting the ship. They needed...her!

It was odd though that they'd chosen a broad-muscled man like Fergus to fetch her.

And it was odd, she pondered, as she followed him up the stairs, that she didn't hear the sounds of fighting. She'd heard noises early on, but now everything seemed still.

Perhaps the other vessel wasn't filled with pirates.

She turned sharply to Fergus. "What is going on?"

"I can't tell you, sir. All a mystery to me, it is. They be wanting to speak to some girl. But we don't 'ave one on board. I would know," Fergus said. "Wish there were a lassie on board." His voice was mournful, and he turned to Louisa. "Bet you do too."

"Well—" If Louisa had been capable of speech before,

and her mind seemed suddenly foggy, so she wasn't sure at all, she certainly was not capable now.

They wanted her.

She wasn't sure how, but she must have been discovered.

Ice spread through her body, and though she'd never needed the railing before, her fingers clutched hold of it as she followed Fergus up the stairs.

Perhaps he wanted her to be here as proof that no men were on board. But wouldn't the men be conducting a search themselves then? For all they knew there was a swarm of people downstairs.

It *probably* wasn't her family.

That would be, well, that would be very unlikely.

"Louisa!"

She stilled. She recognized her stepfather's brash voice.

Heavens.

This was the West Indies. This was far away from England. Far away from Massachusetts. How had the man ever found her?

"May I come out now?" A higher-pitched voice shrieked and was answered in the affirmative.

Mama?

"Where is my daughter?" Her mother marched over the deck. She appeared more tousled, with not nearly as many layers of attire and jewels draped over her, but she was still quite definitely her mother.

Her mother blinked at her, and then recognition seemed to strike, for she howled. "Louisa. What are you clothed in?"

Louisa smoothed her breeches, and for the first time in a long while, she considered their utter impropriety. Her legs were on display. And she'd been consorting with men for weeks with no chaperon in sight. She felt absurd in her masculine attire.

She'd tried so hard to find some independence, but now, now after it had seemed so close, she'd lost everything. Tears invaded her eyes, and she blinked furiously.

She glanced at Rupert. His face was turned toward her stepfather, and she relaxed. He was here. It would be fine.

Of course it was fine.

And of course she'd done the right thing in coming here.

But dread still surged through her as she stepped toward her stepfather. She still swallowed hard, and—

"It's her!" Another voice, this time with a British accent, sounded.

She blinked. It sounded very much like...Sir Seymour. The father of the man she was supposed to marry.

"Look, son!" The voice continued. "It's your bride. I told you we would find her. Leave it all to Papa, that's what I said, and we found her."

She spotted them.

Her legs wobbled, and she clutched hold of the ledge.

"Yep, it's her," Sir Seymour continued. "Now there are prettier chits, but—"

"Don't insult her," Cecil said at once, as if she were truly going to marry him.

"Louisa," a harsh voice said, and she turned.

A tall, muscular man with hair color that resembled her own scowled.

"Arthur?" Her bottom lip dropped downward, and she had the horrible sensation she was simply blinking.

The man's green eyes, the ones that normally crinkled in pleasure when he saw her, glared.

"What on earth are you doing here?" she stammered.

"I think the appropriate thing to ask is what are *you* doing here," Arthur said. "You're fortunate our stepfather came to find me in Falmouth."

"And attired in that outrageous getup." Her stepfather heaved a heavy sigh, one unfortunately not shrouded by either waves or wind. He adjusted his spectacles. "I recognize that shirt. *And* those breeches."

Her heart thumped wildly, as if willing her to flee, but there was nowhere to go.

Her dream had ended, and the man she loved, the man who'd fought pirates and merchants with ease, was giving her up.

"They didn't think we would find you," Sir Seymour interrupted her stepfather's continued admonishments, his voice gleeful. "But I told 'em we would catch you. Finding chits is sort of like hunting."

"Father can shoot pheasants for hours each day," Cecil explained.

"Enough chatter," her stepfather said. "We should go. Get in the vessel!"

"You mean Mr. Thornton's a girl?" Fergus's astonished voice rang out behind her, and she cringed.

Her stepfather pulled the ribbon from her hair, and her queue unraveled. The wind brushed against her locks, lifting them up, in a fashion likely not able to be described as masculine.

"Chit never did have much of a bosom," Sir Seymour declared, and Louisa's cheeks heated with such force, she wouldn't have been surprised if they'd sailed into Hades itself. Her body stiffened, as if each limb was separate from the other, resembling some improperly constructed puppet.

The sailors gawked, their eyebrows raised, and their mouths widened.

"I don't understand," Fergus said slowly.

She softened her voice. "I'm so sorry for not telling you."

Fergus clutched onto his cap, as if ascertaining that his head was still intact. "But you don't look like a girl."

Her legs wobbled, and tears toppled down her cheeks, right before everyone, sealing her humiliation.

"Oh, she does," Rupert's lovely, baritone voice boomed behind her.

Footsteps strode toward her, and her nerves tingled in that now familiar fashion whenever she was in his presence.

She turned toward him, but his gaze remained grim, and his eyes didn't linger on her. They clouded every bit as opaque as that of a sculpture or one of the paintings she'd first thought he belonged in.

Rupert cleared his throat and turned in the direction of her family. "I was shocked to discover the fact. I assure you I had no idea when she boarded the ship that she was not in fact a man."

Humiliation had never surged through her with such strength.

"I can assure you Miss Carmichael was completely taken care of on board," Rupert continued. "The men never even discovered her identity."

"That's for sure," Fergus assented loudly, and she wished he were not nearly as accomplished at raising his voice over the waves. "Never would have guessed. Not in a million billion years."

She'd been swarmed with emotions, enhanced by the sea and the sunshine. She'd thought... Her cheeks flamed further. Well, she certainly hadn't thought that after all those nights in the captain's bedroom, all his protective gestures, that he would be standing before her stepfather and telling him it was a mistake she'd ever gotten on board.

He'd called her to all these people, even though he knew her attire would be found scandalous.

"Do you just mean to give me over to them?" She whispered fiercely to Rupert. "Just like that?"

His face was rigid, almost unrecognizable, and his gaze never met her own. It was foolish to hope, not when the Rupert she'd known appeared so different from this man, but when he nodded in affirmation, her mind did not cease swirling.

"I'm no good for you, darling girl. It's better this way," he whispered. "The ocean is no place for a woman. And they came all this way—they'll take care of you, you'll see."

She was vaguely conscious of people murmuring around her. Somebody was ushering her to the other vessel. She blinked hard.

"Goodbye," Rupert said.

"Goodbye," she stammered. She turned to him, but his eyes were fixed to the horizon, as if the faint smattering of clouds were more interesting.

He was likely relieved to be rid of her so quickly.

Goodness. Had he just used her for his pleasure?

He'd used her for his pleasure. Like those horrible pamphlets like *Matchmaking for Wallflowers* warned women of?

It had been exactly like that.

And she'd thought of marriage. No wonder the man had seemed uncomfortable.

She blinked hard.

"Why were you dressed as a man?" Fergus called after her.

"To protect her virtue," Rupert said at once.

"See!" Sir Seymour elbowed Cecil. "Your bride is still virtuous! What did I tell you? I knew it was good to go after her? Papa knows best."

She stared at the sea below her as she moved over the plank that joined the two ships, at least temporarily. The waves seemed to urge the ships to separate.

It was only later she realized that she'd left her research on *The Sapphire Princess.*

Her chest tightened, but she struggled to think of a reason why she should dash after it.

Everything had changed.

She was going to get married. To Cecil. Just like before.

She'd had her holiday, she'd met the man she loved... But he didn't love her back.

She blinked hard.

*

Rupert watched Louisa descend the ship, taking his heart with her. Remaining firm had taken huge amounts of reserve.

But she couldn't stay here. It wouldn't be decent. The West Indies was a dangerous place. It was no place for a woman. Arthur was right.

"Let's go," he said to the sailors. "We're still bound for Falmouth."

The sailors blinked at him.

"I can't believe that she was a woman all this time," one person moaned.

"Of course, she was," Rupert said. "And an extremely intelligent one at that." He smiled. "Not that it would have taken extreme amounts of intelligence to fool you lot."

"I think it would have," Fergus insisted, clearly outraged. "I'm sure she would be. Why, I reckon she's the smartest person I've ever met."

He nodded. "I think you might be correct."

He still had memories of her. That would have to suffice. Because he absolutely could not put her in danger. She said she liked the ocean, but it was a passion that many women claimed to have. Many women took pleasure in looking at the various colors and strength of the waves. But that didn't mean that they were suited for life on board a ship.

He'd had to be firm for her.

Because I love her.

He mulled over the thought. Wasn't love supposed to make people happy, and not cause his heart to ache as if a butcher had recently mistaken it for meat?

Chapter
Twenty-three

L ouisa stepped onto the new ship.

An unfamiliar crew pointed in her direction, musing loudly over her. Once again she felt exposed in her breeches, conscious of every curve, or lack of curve, the tight fabric revealed.

She moved gingerly over the new deck. How was it possible for it to resemble the other ship, yet differ so entirely?

Someone was washing the deck, but the person's rags were the wrong color, and the spaces between the steps were the wrong length.

Louisa strove to raise her chin, even though the task seemed to demand a strength found more commonly in wrestlers. She strove to keep tears from flooding her eyes.

She tried to smile. It shouldn't have been so easy to disguise herself. There seemed to be no greater sign.

"Young lady!" Her stepfather's brash voice barked at

her. "You gave your mother quite a fright. You could have been killed."

"Or worse," her mother shrieked, clasping her heart.

"I—I'm sorry." She hadn't wanted to cause anyone pain. But her last few weeks had seemed to show that there was no greater sign that she was unsuited to a life filled with dresses and coiffures. "I left a note."

"Knowing where you are located is not enough to keep your mother from worrying. Not when the only women who venture alone on ships are whores."

She tensed. She'd never heard that word from her stepfather's lips before, but he smiled, as if taking glee in the fact that he'd managed to shock her. "Your maid told us you boarded the ship the day before you went missing. We went straight to Arthur, and we were lucky the man was able to track down *The Sapphire Princess*—your brother was surprisingly good at finding it. At least one of your mother's children made me proud."

"Oh." She glanced over at her brother, but Arthur had fixed his face into a scowling expression. Clearly no one was forgiving her anytime soon.

"You're lucky I had this vessel with me," her stepfather continued. "You're also exceedingly lucky that Mr. Amberly remains willing to take you on. Most men wouldn't."

"You should be happy to be off that boat," Sir Seymour said. "Land is much better. Much less swirling about."

"The two experiences are quite different," Louisa said solemnly. At one point she may have laughed at her future father-in-law's staunch idiocy.

Sir Seymour nodded rapidly. "Clever chit. Clever chit indeed. Knew there had to be some advantages to your appearance. Can't be too careful about poor traits getting into the bloodline."

Louisa smiled tightly.

"Good thing we rescued you," Sir Seymour mused. "Good thing indeed. Could have had actual pirates get to you. That would have been tragic indeed." He smoothed his frock coat. "I rather think the Duke of Alfriston might see me quite favorably now. Quite favorably indeed."

"How marvelous for you," she said, her voice cold. She glanced at the others, but they had drifted farther away from her. Her new fiancé seemed more interested in reading a book, and Arthur and her stepfather still scowled whenever they caught her gaze.

"The Duke and I are, you know, great friends." Sir Seymour leaned in closer to her, and some strange floral concoction wafted over her. Clearly the baronet had not gone without his cologne. "I think it's because we are both very important men in the region. What with both being aristocrats and all."

"My brother's estate is in Sussex. Yours is in Yorkshire."

The man didn't even blush, even though she was sure that he must have at one point glanced at a map and noticed that the two counties were separated by hundreds of miles filled with hills, rivers, and large cities.

"His wife is my niece." Sir Seymour didn't exactly pound his chest, but his hand did come very near that region, and his torso swelled with what she could only assume was pride.

Louisa frowned. Her brother and sister-in-law certainly had not seemed equally effusive about this neighbor and relative.

"Obviously, we are as close as can be. And now with

my son marrying the duke's sister..." Sir Seymour smiled fondly. "Well, I'm sure all the *ton* can forgive my son for choosing a woman of some eccentricity. But that's what happens when your brother only has one leg. These things happen. People will understand."

Louisa blinked. "My brother's injury is not—"

"Something that should be discussed." Arthur strode toward them.

"I agree," Louisa said.

"Sensible woman." Sir Seymour raised his voice and turned in the direction of his son. "Cecil, did you hear that I think you've picked yourself a good woman?"

"Er, yes," Cecil said loyally.

"It's that great taste that made him wait to choose one," Sir Seymour said proudly.

"How extraordinary to find that you chased me so far," Louisa said.

"Well. We are happy to cultivate a romantic instinct in our son. The man reads so much poetry! And he prides himself on his fashion," Sir Seymour boasted. "You would think he was Brummel's shadow. The way his gaze followed Brummel's back where ever the man turned."

"Just admiring the man's fabric choices," Cecil said. His face was pinker than it had been previously, and Louisa pondered her new husband-to-be.

"I'll make you happy," Cecil said more seriously as if reading her mind. "I'll give you the freedom to do your research. Your maid explained to me how passionate you were about it."

"She did?" Louisa smiled. "That was kind of her."

Cecil grinned, and Louisa's shoulders relaxed. "I'll honor your desires," he continued. "If you want to live in America, or here—"

"Well, you should get around to having babies," Sir Seymour said.

Cecil shrugged. "Whatever my wife desires. I can't promise her everything, but—if she wants to do research, she can."

It was kind of the man.

It was certainly more than she'd hoped for in a match.

She'd always yearned for romance, but never, in fact, expected it.

Veronique seemed to be sufficiently romantic for both of them.

And now she would marry, be rid of her mother's frenzied search for a fiancé for her, and she would still be able to do the research she'd always longed to do.

It should have been everything.

It should have been happiness itself.

She glanced at *The Sapphire Princess* as it cut through the waves, some distance away. The tall masts adorned with billowing sails made something in her heart ache.

She sucked in a breath of the salty sea air and forced herself to smile at Cecil. "I appreciate your words ever so much. Now I must retire."

"Sure thing!" Sir Seymour said cheerfully. "Must be upsetting for a girl like you, a sister of a duke, to be forced to live in such reduced circumstances. One at least wants to stride on a ground that isn't swaying. The good Lord created ground for us to walk upon most of the time. Don't see why sailors have to abandon it."

"Mmm-hmm."

"You'll probably be spending the whole night crying tears of joy." Sir Seymour beamed again. "But it's all right. My son is here to marry you. Your temporary insanity has been forgiven!"

Louisa nodded, not trusting her voice to remain steady were she to attempt to speak. She rushed to the accommodations and tried to feel grateful that they weren't on sea, but she couldn't muster any joy at all.

Somehow she'd always thought Rupert would fight for her. She'd been prepared to fight alongside him when she thought the other boat contained pirates, and not her relatives and relatives-to-be.

All he needed to tell them was that he wanted her to stay. That he didn't want her to marry Cecil. That he wanted to marry...her.

But the notion was infantile. Rupert was happy sailing on his own with his crew finding diversions at every port.

Perhaps her mother had been right. Perhaps Louisa had had it all wrong, all along. Perhaps she should have focused on her appearance. Perhaps it had been foolish for her to focus on her research. Perhaps it should have simply been a hobby as everyone condescendingly suggested.

For though she'd never mentioned the word love, she had no doubt that that was what she felt. And though she could not force Rupert to feel similarly, she'd thrown away her reputation and any future chances of love.

Cecil was kind, but even he admitted nervously that he would never be a husband prone to the more typical passions. And even though such a marriage would once have seemed tolerable, she now longed for... *More.*

She'd never again meet Rupert's eyes; she'd never again feel his arms wrap around her, and she'd never again hear the sound of his laughter.

Her features grew rigid, and she locked the door to her cabin. She sank to her floor, wrapping her arms around her chest, as if it might protect her heart from breaking.

But it was no use.

It already had.

*

She was gone.

Her quarters were empty, and no slender figure with thick auburn hair lay pressed against him when he woke.

Memories of watching Louisa being hauled off invaded his mind.

She hadn't wanted to leave. Her face had been so pale, her gray eyes so wide, and her shoulders had tensed so much. Guilt ratcheted through him.

It was for the best. Her own brother had said so, and Arthur had worked with him for years. He knew Rupert's faults, his lies, better than anyone else.

He had to let her go. Her relatives might be eccentric, but they were well-intentioned. They cared for her, and they would keep her safe. Cecil Amberly could bring his bride to some manor house, and keep her ensconced from all the real pirates that roamed the Caribbean, all the diseases, all the storms.

Yet his guilt did not abate.

He vowed to at least bring her research to her and strode through his quarters. He avoided glancing at the sofa and dining room table, as if averting his gaze from the areas where Louisa had sat and laughed might banish the painful memories that flooded through his mind with a force more commonly found in typhoons.

He strode to her room and opened the door to her cabin. Her diving helmet lay on the table, and he sighed. He would need to give it to her. He knew how important it was for her.

He ran his hand over the material, pondering how long it must have taken to design and get the costume made.

It was incredible.

Most incredible.

A person who did that had more than a passing passion for the ocean.

A person who might actually want to spend her life on a ship.

Just like him.

Blast. She'd attempted to tell him. She'd tried to reason with him. But he'd been too thick-headed to realize the veracity of her statements. He'd dismissed her desires, just as everyone else did, even when he claimed to want to protect her. He'd given in too much to his fears, even though he prided in choosing a life of bravery for himself.

He grabbed hold of her journal. He was aware he was breaking all sorts of protocol, but he needed to be sure.

He read through her research. Through every painstakingly recorded detail.

The woman was incredible.

And he'd tossed her aside.

His chest tightened as if some boa constrictor had slithered over from the shore and wrapped itself around him. What must she think?

He rose abruptly and stuffed the journal into his satchel. His heart thumped wildly, but he wasn't going to linger to give it time to recover now.

There was one thing it needed.

One thing *he* needed.

Louisa.

And she was about to get married to some pale Englishman who wouldn't love her.

He refused to permit that.

He rushed from her cabin, and the door slammed behind him. The noise boomed through the corridor, and more than one sailor hollered at him.

"You fine, Cap'n?" Fergus asked.

He smiled. He'd never been so miserable in all his life.

But maybe, just maybe he could change that.

"I'm going out, Fergus."

The man blinked. "You're gonna go to that wedding?"

"What?"

Fergus grinned. "Some of the crew was talking about it, Cap'n. Heard about it at the public house. Mighty fast, ain't it?"

His stomach tumbled down. "I suppose the marital laws are laxer here."

Fergus laughed. "Apparently they got the Archbishop of Canterbury's permission himself before they left. Fancy that. We was talking with someone who knew the archbishop!"

"What time is the wedding?" he asked carefully.

"Reckon you'll just about make it," the man said. "If you run."

Damnation.

"Don't be too horrified," Fergus said hastily. "You can run. I've seen you do it!" He sighed. "Just pretend there are pirates coming after you. Or Americans, before the war stopped, and you had to be nice to them again."

"Yes."

Fergus scrutinized him. "Might I suggest, sir, that you wear a jacket? Those pasty Englishmen might think it a bit odd that you're not wearing a shirt. What with it being a wedding and all. And what with them being pasty. Reckon the sun's never set its rays on their skin."

Rupert remembered to breathe. "I didn't think you would give me fashion advice."

Fergus shrugged sheepishly. "It's okay, sir. I know yer jes like me. Your accent's just a bit nicer, but reckon it must be jes as strange for you as me. What with being sold into the navy at such a young age." Fergus shook his head mournfully.

Damnation. The familiar guilt swirled through him, and he rushed to his quarters.

"Getting yer shirt?" Fergus called after him.

"Yes." But as he hastily pulled it over him, he also grabbed his letter.

He'd been too secretive.

He was going to change that.

He was going to change everything.

Chapter
Twenty-four

H er brother had arranged for one of the local women to do her hair, and Louisa sat in a chair as the person brushed her locks. A dress hung on the door.

My wedding dress.

It was plainer than anything she would have worn in England, but it seemed Sir Seymour was not going to allow another chance for her to escape.

Not that she would. She'd thought Rupert had cared for her, but she'd never been so mistaken.

Sir Seymour strolled toward them. His top hat gleamed under the strong sunbeams shining through the window.

"You're about to be married." The woman smiled as if that was the only possible reaction to those words. "I love weddings."

"Ah, yes!" Her mother clapped her hands.

Louisa laughed weakly, but if her mother noticed the weak strength of her laughter, she didn't remark on it, and her own laugh barreled forcefully enough for both of them.

"Are you certain it would not be better to wait until we return?" Louisa asked.

"We must go to the church," she said, and Cecil nodded.

He looked as nervous and as uncomfortable as she did. She sighed. She could have worse husbands.

She tried to push away the thought that she could also have a better one.

But Rupert would be firmly relegated to the past, as dreamlike as the turquoise water they'd floated on, and the palm trees that fluttered even now in the breeze.

*

Rupert ran through *The Sapphire Princess*.

"Something wrong, Cap'n?" one sailor shouted at him.

"Bloody everything!"

The sailor's eyes widened, and Rupert called out. "But carry on. As normal." What did his heart mean to these men?

He ran to where the shore boat should be. Where it always was.

Where it bloody well wasn't now.

He cursed, and Fergus strode up to him. "What's the matter, Cap'n?"

Rupert gestured to the water. "The boat. The boat is not there. And I need to go on shore. I need to stop—"

"The boat's on the shore now. Reckon it will be back soon."

Rupert swallowed hard. He didn't have time for soon. He needed to stop a wedding.

How long did ceremonies normally last? Certainly nobody else but him was planning to speak up or forever hold his peace.

He tossed the packet to Fergus. "When the boat returns, you go to the chapel. With these."

He blinked. "Of course, Captain Rosse."

Rupert couldn't remember the last time the man had called him Captain Rosse. At least he seemed to have some idea of the magnitude of his task.

"I'll be there soon," Fergus said.

"Me too," Rupert said curtly. He clambered to the top of the railing. He noticed Fergus's mouth start to part, but he didn't wait to see how low it would fall.

He knew he never ever dove. The last time he'd been submerged in water was because Americans were shooting at him and because the ship had collapsed beneath him. The last time he'd been submerged, Jasper had died and—

He mustn't think of that. He sucked in a deep breath of air and dove over the ledge.

A splash sounded, and he realized it was himself, sinking into the ocean. The water wrapped around him, rippling around him like an icy blanket.

"Captain?" Fergus's voice sounded, muffled in the distance, and Rupert remembered that he needed to kick his feet, needed to move his hands, needed to *swim* to get to Louisa. To save her. To save himself.

He forced himself to swim upward, kicking away the plants that grew in the ocean.

One thought was in his mind:

Louisa.

He had to—*had to*—get there in time.

He still swam, and after fewer than a hundred strokes

he touched the land. He'd never been so happy to be in Falmouth.

Sunbeams splattered over his face, and he squinted into the bright light and sprinted toward the chapel.

He wished he'd not taken the time to put on a shirt. What if she was already wed? It wouldn't matter how fancy the ruffles of his shirt were then.

Not that he would look anything but a mess now.

Toward Louisa.

Toward his...*love*.

He was vaguely aware of the locals blinking up at him in bemusement, peering at him as they hauled crates of sugar to the other ships in the port.

He firmed his lips and was grateful when his feet pounded against the firmly packed dirt that signified he'd arrived at the main road of the town.

He wove through wheelbarrows and more locals. And finally he dashed up the stairs of the chapel, pushed open the door of the chapel, and...

His chest tightened.

They were there. They all were. Sir Seymour, Mr. Amberly, Mr. and Mrs. Daventry, Arthur Carmichael and his own Louisa.

They all seemed to notice that he was there too.

"What on earth?" Sir Seymour's voice thundered through the chapel, the sound amplified by the evident carefulness the architects had taken in the room's acoustics so that even the most mild-mannered minister's whispers would confront the congregation with the force of a cannon ball firing into enemy soldiers.

"Stop the wedding!" Rupert shouted.

The people did not seem less confused. He looked at Louisa, but even she seemed startled to see him.

Never mind that now. He stumbled toward her, only now becoming aware of the ridiculousness of his appearance. He brushed seaweed from his attire, and water dripped onto the aisle.

"Are you married yet?" he asked.

His heart stopped, fear halting even the routine process of breathing, but then her voice came out, strong and steady as ever. "I'm not."

Relief surged through him.

Chapter
Twenty-five

They weren't married yet, but they would be soon.

What on earth was *Rupert* doing here?

Louisa stared at him.

Did he intend to watch? The word scythed through her, and she blinked, as if the motion might succeed in halting the tears that threatened to spread through her.

This was her wedding. She didn't need Rupert here to disturb it. She would only have one, and she didn't want to spend the short time thinking about someone who wasn't the groom.

Even if the groom was likely not thinking any romantic thoughts about her.

"I think you should leave," Louisa said.

His expression sobered, but he strode nearer her. Lord help her, but she couldn't stop herself from pondering his natural swagger, the breadth of his shoulders and the stubble on his face that hinted that their time apart just may, just possibly, have affected him too.

He ambled toward her, and his blue eyes were pleading. She looked away and tried to focus on Cecil's bland expression, contentedly bemused that an uninvited guest, the same one who had spent weeks alone with his wife-to-be, was here before them.

"You don't have to do this," Rupert said.

He was wrong. It was kind of him to desire to imbue her with self-confidence to live life on her own, but she'd tried that before. If she didn't marry Cecil, it would have to be someone else. She shuddered to think who such a future husband would be, likely bribed heavily by her stepfather to temper the effects of her utter disregard of her reputation and her complete absence of respectability if she ever returned to Massachusetts in an unmarried state.

"You don't understand," she said. "I do." She tried to smile at Cecil. She needed to make him see that she would be happy. She didn't want him to worry about her. She needed to make him see that everything would be fine and that he shouldn't feel guilty for not loving her.

Her throat dried.

She wished they served water at ceremonies like this.

"You should leave," Sir Seymour said, his voice cold.

Perhaps she suspected something after all. Perhaps, even when her heart was broken, even when Rupert signified everything that made pain tumble through her body, perhaps even still, she drank him in, as if he meant everything to her.

Even when he was never supposed to mean anything but a casual, very temporary break from the constraints of society.

He'd been an adventure, and adventures had no place at anything so solemn as a wedding.

"I can't leave," Rupert said. "Not without making an offer to Miss Carmichael."

His voice was solemn, his gaze serious, but she told herself that she couldn't hope that he felt anything toward her. She couldn't hope that he returned any of her feelings, for that wouldn't change that he didn't want her by his side.

He needed to leave.

Instead he dropped to the floor, kneeling in the aisle. His face remained solemn, but something like nervousness seemed to reach his eyes. "Miss Louisa Carmichael will you do me the honor of becoming my wife?"

"But she's marrying someone else," Sir Seymour shrieked, his voice reaching an unmanly height. "Can't you see?"

"Let him speak," Cecil said, smiling.

Louisa smiled back. She blinked, but Rupert was still there, still kneeling right in the middle of the aisle, right in the middle of the church, right in the middle of her wedding.

"I am completely and utterly in love with you," Rupert said, his voice gaining strength.

He loves me.

Rupert's words rushed over her like a warm, blissful wave. Her legs trembled, as if she were sinking into the sand, but the firm rock of the church floor was beneath her.

This is real.

"Please forgive me," Rupert said. "I should never have let you go yesterday. I'm so, so sorry. Please give me the chance to make that up to you for the rest of my life. I—I beg you."

"So it doesn't matter that you're a captain?" she asked uncertainly.

"I'll take you with me," Rupert promised, and Louisa's heart expanded. "Perhaps we can stop eventually, but I know you love the ocean. I should never have made the decision without you."

Louisa's heart swelled further, and she gazed at Rupert, still kneeling on the stone cobbles.

"It's fine," Cecil whispered beside her. "I won't mind. I promise."

"I'm sorry," she whispered back.

"It's better this way. For both of us." He grinned and glanced at Rupert again. "Especially for you."

She laughed, and this time she didn't squelch the joy that cascaded through her.

"Thank you," she said, and then gestured to Rupert. "Come here."

"Wait!" her mother exclaimed. "I don't know who this...sea captain is, but he certainly is not marrying my oldest daughter."

Louisa blinked.

She hadn't anticipated resistance. The happiness that had surged through her halted abruptly. She didn't need his permission, but she very much desired it.

"A sea captain is not such an unworthy occupation," she said carefully. "Mr. Daventry was one too after all."

"Our stepfather was not the kind of captain this man was," Arthur interjected.

Rupert's face paled, but he still strode toward them. "I love her. I will take care of her. I promise."

"The profession shows definite skill and business acumen," Louisa continued. "Indeed many of Salem's highest bred men are captains and—"

"The profession is still not as good as someone who doesn't have to work at all," Sir Seymour interrupted. "Like my Cecil. Never worked a day in his life. Couldn't make a father prouder."

"We have an agreement with the baronet and his son," her stepfather continued. "We should honor it. How can you give up your chance to converse regularly with English royalty?"

"Well, my father is simply a baronet," Cecil said carefully, but her stepfather and mother stormed from the church.

Louisa's heart sank. She rushed after them, picking up her skirts to not trip over the long fabric.

*

Rupert followed Louisa from the chapel. His feet pounded over the tilestones, still wet from his entrance. The others shouted behind him, but he focused his attention on Louisa.

She was dressed in a dress which he could only assume she'd borrowed from her mother. But she was the most beautiful being he'd ever seen, she always was.

He pushed open the doors to the chapel and exited. He squinted into the bright light, conscious of the shouts of the locals.

"Cap'n!" One of his sailors shouted at him, and he turned his gaze, puzzled.

He'd anticipated Fergus, but they'd all come. The fact made him smile until he remembered that there would be nothing to smile about unless Louisa agreed to marry him.

Which he felt much less certain about.

He was certain women weren't supposed to flee from the men who'd just proposed to them.

"I know you're reluctant to let me marry your stepdaughter," Rupert said.

"You're just a sea captain." Mrs. Daventry's nose wrinkled in distaste, and Rupert suspected there were better times to compare himself to her husband.

"I think your wife would be pacified to know I'm not merely a sea captain."

Louisa's eyes widened, and she shook her head. "You—you don't need to speak of that."

"I do. I should have long ago."

"Look," Mr. Daventry said. "I know that you were taken from your home when you were just a child. I know you've been spending your whole life on ships. And that's good... For you. But that's not good for my oldest stepdaughter. And I cannot, simply cannot permit a match. No matter how sharp your rise to captaining a ship of your own."

"I lied before," Rupert said.

Louisa looked saddened. "You don't have to tell him—"

"I know exactly where I came from," Rupert said. "Even if I don't always like it. Even if my father was nothing to emulate."

"I knew it," Mr. Daventry said. "I knew you were just some over-sized street urchin."

"My father has done much wrong in the world." Rupert grimaced, thinking about how the man had loaned money to peers, and then sent henchmen after them to pay the exorbitant interest. Dukes did not answer to the law like other people did, and his father had always taken full advantage of that. He sighed. "But I am not, nor was I ever, a street urchin. My title was quite different."

"Well, it's to be of a higher status than a street urchin," Mr. Daventry grumbled. "But that certainly does not mean—"

"I am a duke," he said quickly.

Mr. Daventry blinked. The others were busy gasping and looking shocked.

Rupert shifted his legs over the uneven sand. It was a reaction he was accustomed to receiving as a youth. It was a reaction he had observed so often that he'd vowed after he'd been presumed dead, after he'd been given a chance to choose his own life, never to tell anyone again. He didn't want to ponder whether the reason for his rise as a sea captain was because of some merchants' desires to gain favor with his father.

"*You* claim to be a *duke?*" Sarcasm rippled through Mr. Daventry's voice.

"That's a clever thing to say!" Fergus said a moment later. The man put his arm around Rupert. "Yep, the man's a duke."

Rupert appreciated the man's sentiment. Even if it was obvious he didn't believe a word of it. Neither did Mr. Daventry.

"Ah..." Sir Seymour cleared his throat noisily. "Though I appreciate that you were inspired by my aristocratic appearance to feign being an aristocrat yourself, you forget that we are too clever to believe you."

"I thought that," Rupert said.

Sir Seymour beamed. "For a man born on the streets, you possess a shrivel of intelligence."

"Perhaps it was one of the nicer streets," Cecil said, his

eyes twinkling more than he thought possible for a man whose bride was about to be stolen from him.

Sir Seymour laughed. "You're right, Cecil. It must have been one of the nicer streets. Near Parliament perhaps?"

"I was not born near Parliament," Rupert said. "I was born in Hampshire. My father was the last Duke of Belmonte. And I am—"

"His son!" Cecil gazed at him in shock. "I thought I recognized you."

"Oh, that's why you kept on glancing at him." Sir Seymour clapped his hands together and then turned to Rupert. "You were lost at sea."

Cecil's cheeks pinkened. "Er—indeed."

"So all this time..."

"While your parents thought you dead," Sir Seymour's voice was stern. "You were alive!"

Rupert looked down. His parents had known he was alive. He'd been imprisoned by the Americans for longer than he desired to ponder, but once he'd been freed, he'd written to them and told them he would retire after exploring the area a bit longer. He couldn't face the crowd at Almack's or White's, when his best friend had died, when he'd seen real war. And when he learned more of his father's corruption, the stories traveling all the way to the West Indies, his desire to stay had only strengthened.

His parents hadn't understood his desire to stay. They'd only been ashamed of him.

And so he'd remained in the West Indies, and they'd continued to call him dead, too embarrassed to admit that he'd spent time imprisoned by a people generally viewed as incompetent. He'd told people he had no parents, and they'd assumed he'd been impressed into the navy, like so many others.

"You're really a duke?" Fergus asked, his eyes wide.

"Truly."

Fergus dropped his hand from his shoulder immediately. "I don't even know how to call you."

"Captain is fine," he said. "Or my given name, if you desire to tease me."

"Ah," Sir Seymour said, and Rupert's shoulders stiffened. "I might have some opinions on that matter. I'm well-acquainted with dukes. In fact my niece married a duke herself. And my other niece married an earl. He actually used to visit me when still unmarried. Lord Somerville, I'm sure you've heard of him."

Fergus blinked, but Sir Seymour continued. "The man had the option of choosing between all the great pleasures of London, all the delights thrust upon a handsome, aristocratic man, but he chose to while away his time in my house." Sir Seymour smiled. "I am more entertaining than all the *ton* put together! It is a great honor that you all had the pleasure of meeting me."

The others shifted their legs and seemed preoccupied with gazing at the ocean.

"Did you know he was a duke?" Mrs. Daventry asked Louisa loudly. "Can it really be true?"

"It's true," Louisa said. "I didn't know his father had passed away, but I knew he would inherit."

"And I have the papers to prove it," Rupert said hastily. "It's not just a chance likeness with a long passed away warrior." He nodded to Fergus. "If I could have the satchel."

The man handed it to him hastily and then gave him a quick bow. He turned to Sir Seymour.

"Was that deep enough?" Fergus asked.

"In your position I would go deeper. Much deeper.

He's far more important than you," Sir Seymour explained, and Rupert did his best to avoid strangling the man. "Remember to call him Your Grace," Sir Seymour continued.

"Right," Fergus said.

"You don't need to say those things," Rupert said. "That's not why I revealed my birth. It was simply to win Miss Carmichael's hand. I am completely and utterly in love with your daughter."

Louisa's cheeks pinkened, and her mouth parted, and her eyes shone. "I love you too."

Rupert beamed and pulled her toward him. "My darling."

"Louisa?" Her mother opened her mouth. "I don't know what to say, I—"

"Just say we can marry, Mama," Louisa said.

Her mother's lips moved upward. "Very well."

Rupert grinned and pressed her to him, soaking her body against his wet attire, and kissed her.

"My darling, Louisa."

And life was more wonderful than ever before.

Epilogue

Excerpt from *Matchmaking for Wallflowers*
July 1818

All of London is excited.

The new Duke of Belmonte is arriving—but readers, he will be captaining a ship. *The Sapphire Princess* is headed to our delightful port, and even the finest ladies of the *ton* are inquiring on the safest spots on the Embankment to greet him and his new wife.

Young debutantes, take heart, the Duchess of Belmonte (née Carmichael) proved our editors wrong. Even in the highest strata of aristocrats, even in the most refined ranks of Harrow-educated warriors, it may be possible to find a man who will listen to your rambles on obscure facts. Even if your passion is...fish.

Though the Duke of Belmonte may be excused for his unconventional marriage by the absence of competing female company, we are assured by the very best sources that their affection is unfeigned.

We have been privileged to interview Sir Seymour,

a baronet who assures us of his utter respectability in Yorkshire, that mysterious province to the North, where only the brave or societally challenged venture.

We lamented with him that his only son, Mr. Cecil Amberly, has sworn off future marriages. Mr. Amberly's first intended fiancée is now the Duchess of Alfriston, and his second intended fiancée is now the Duchess of Belmonte. We cry with him that tragedy has so frequently befallen him in his pursuit of love. Fortunately he is being distracted by various young dandies who frequent the theater. Though the conversation of these fashion-adoring young men must make a poor substitution for that of the country's preeminent archaeologist and marine biologist, the man is at least showing a brave face, and we have not once seen him without a wide smile.

The English are the bravest people in this world, and it is tragic that there is no war currently for them to show their valor. Still, we are certain the debutantes are grateful for the abundance of men at balls, even if the plight of the few wallflowers remains puzzling and less excusable.

Perhaps they will learn some wisdom from the former Miss Carmichael, a woman we pride ourselves in that we pointed out her eccentricities to you, our dearest readers. She has landed a duke though we mourn with her that she has been forced to accompany the Duke of Belmonte on all his journeys. Even wives of other, less aristocratic captains expressed surprise that she'd elected to spend her life on a rocking ship rather than in a house that looked over the ocean on stable ground. We can only surmise that Americans lack any conventionality.

Though some merchants claim to refuse to work with the Duke of Belmonte, seeing his new bride's presence on the ship as a potential target for kidnappers, one suspects that they may be merely jealous. The vast majority of merchants seem to delight in telling their acquaintances of their business dealings with a duke.

We at *Matchmaking for Wallflowers* will be mingling with the crowd on the Embankment. Fear not readers, we remain anonymous. There is a special joy that fills the minds of the most confirmed cynics when they witness true love, and every merchant has assured us that their love is genuine.

Take heart, wallflowers. Have hope, and if all else fails, you may consider stealing your servants' breeches.

About Bianca

Born in Texas, Wellesley graduate Bianca Blythe spent four years in England. She worked in a fifteenth century castle though sadly that didn't actually involve spotting dukes and earls strutting about in Hessians.

She credits British weather for forcing her into a library, where she discovered her first Julia Quinn novel. She remains deeply grateful for blustery downpours.

Bianca lives in Massachusetts with her dashing rogue.

*

Other books in the *Matchmaking for Wallflowers* series:
How to Capture a Duke
A Rogue to Avoid
Runaway Wallflower
Mad About the Baron
A Marquess for Convenience

Made in the USA
Lexington, KY
25 May 2018